Long Live Life!

LONG LIVE LIFE!

Alphonse Allais

Translated and with an introduction & notes
by Doug Skinner

BLACK SCAT BOOKS
2017

LONG LIVE LIFE!

by Alphonse Allais

Translated from the French by Doug Skinner

Copyright © 2017, 2018 by Black Scat Books

Translation, notes, and illustration © 2017, 2018 by Doug Skinner

ISBN-13 978-0-9992622-4-5

Cover & book design by Norman Conquest

Frontispiece: illustration by Doug Skinner

ACKNOWLEDGEMENTS:

This collection was originally published in France in 1892 under the title *Vive la vie !*

The story "Shocking" originally appeared in *Le Scat Noir* #228.

Facing page: silhouette of the author with noisemaker

BLACK SCAT BOOKS

Sublime Art & Literature

BlackScatBooks.net

CONTENTS

NO SOPHOMORE SLUMP
FOR THIS BOHEMIAN

This is, I believe, the seventh book by Alphonse Allais that I've translated for Black Scat Books. That makes the seventh introduction, too. Some repetition is unavoidable, and I hope returning readers will wait patiently while I orient newcomers.

Alphonse Allais was born on October 20, 1874, in the Norman town of Honfleur. His father ran the town pharmacy; consequently, after a childhood not particularly distinguished by either academic achievement or spirited rebellion, young Alphonse was sent to Paris to study pharmacy.

Paris, however, offered its usual temptations of cabarets, cafes, and Parisiennes; the budding druggist quickly became a budding Bohemian. He started contributing to the many ephemeral publications that continually sprang up in Paris, providing squibs and jokes to such papers as *Le Tintamarre*, *L'Hydropathe*, and *L'Anti-Concierge*. Even at the start, he favored wordplay and formal conceits, channeling his jokes into forms like the fable-express (a verse with a punning moral), the *comble* (a one-liner defining the "utmost" of something), or the autograph (a pun on a famous name).

He soon settled into Le Chat Noir, the cabaret founded by Rodolphe Salis, renowned for its medieval decor and Salis's spirited abuse of his customers. It also became known for featuring lively young poets and singers, and for elaborate shadow plays concocted by gifted painters, cartoonists, and composers. In the best Bohemian tradition, everyone was paid in aperitifs, if at all. Allais obligingly whacked a drum for the shadow plays, and wrote monologues for the resident monologist, Coquelin Cadet. He acquired a reputation for wild imagination, bold pranks, and deadpan delivery. He was pale and blond, with a trim beard and Norman reserve; more than one memoir compared him to an English schoolmaster.

The Chat Noir also published a weekly and eponymous paper, brimming with poems, stories, gossip, cartoons, and other byproducts of Bohemian life. Allais experimented with a number of forms, including verses, monologues, parodies, and short stories, both serious and comic. He had abandoned his studies somewhere along the way, and turned his stint at the *Chat Noir* into a course in journalism, learning the techniques of topical commentary, hoaxes, and controversy, and mastering the essential art of extending a punchline into a page of copy. He became editor in 1885.

A few of his monologues were published in nice little booklets by Ollendorff; in 1891, the same firm published his first collection, *A se tordre*, drawn from his pieces in *Le Chat Noir* (available, I feel impelled to add, from Black Scat Books in my translation, as *Double Over*). With *A se tordre*, Allais defined himself as a primarily comic writer, specializing in what the French called *loufoquerie*, craziness.

The book sold well, emboldening Allais to leave *Le Chat Noir*, and to accept an offer from a larger and more mainstream paper, *Le Journal*. There he adapted his techniques to a wider readership, and to the shorter format of the newspaper column.

His second book, *Vive la vie!*, which you now have in hand, was published in 1892, just as he was headed for *Le Journal*. He penned the following blurb for *Le Chat Noir*, for the April 30, 1892 issue:

"*Long Live Life!* Such is the anti-Schopenhauerizing title of the new book by our friend and collaborator Alphonse Allais. This volume is and will remain the book of the century.

"One would have to be a pretty contemptible wretch not to go immediately in search of it at Flammarion, which has had the excellent idea to start a series of *Merry Authors*.

"Bravo, Flammarion (Ernest)! Explosions of laughter are better than dynamite.

"Long live life, damn it!"

The second book, like the first, was drawn mostly from his work at *Le Chat Noir*, and can be read as a summation of the genre and style he had developed there. The pieces are mostly short stories, in the same vein as de Maupassant's: light, conversational tales of love, adultery, the supernatural, and military life, often tending to the bawdy. Allais, however, makes them particularly Allaisian by embellishing them with digressions, parenthetical asides, footnotes, puns, topical references, joke names, military jargon, Parisian slang, neologisms, dog Latin, literary quotations, catchphrases, allusions to friends and colleagues, and shameless padding.

All of this is a translator's nightmare. Really, you have no idea. I found English equivalents for the puns, and tried to provide slang that's not anachronistic. Allais's characters usually sport names in three categories: puns, friends, and public figures. After wrestling with my conscience, I decided not to rename those poor characters saddled with puns (although I did make an exception in the case of Colydor). Instead, I discreetly glossed them in the notes. I also identified the real people who pop up here and there.

A few Parisian characters recur often enough to warrant a mention beforehand.

Francisque Sarcey, who becomes somewhat of a running joke throughout, was a prolific drama critic, and the butt of young writers and artists for his middlebrow tastes, loose rambling prose, and rotundity. Montmartre wits liked to mine his columns for unwitting double entendres; Allais characteristically took the mockery further by writing columns under Sarcey's byline. The Allais Sarcey was a lecherous buffoon, boasting of his appetite and complaining about his constipation and impotence. Sarcey, who seems to have been a surprisingly genial sort, claimed to enjoy the youngsters' hijinks, although he must have grown tired of them. He also regularly attended shows at Le Chat Noir, although a special chair had to be built to hold him. (Let me add that Black Scat Books has published my translation of this extended prank as *I Am Sarcey*.)

Léon Gandillot is mentioned a few times; he sang at the Chat Noir, and wrote several successful plays. Perhaps most crucially here, he succeeded Allais as editor of *Le Chat Noir*.

Henri Gauthier-Villars also appears a couple of times, although in "The New Boating" he's nominally disguised as "Villier-Gauthars." Better known under the *nom de journaliste* Willy, he generated reams of music criticism and stacks of novels, mostly written by a staff of ghostwriters, chief among them his wife Colette. He and Allais were fellow members of the Zutiste circle that gathered around the poet and inventor Charles Cros, and competed for the attentions of the tiny and tempestuous Charlotte Kinceler.

The populist politician General Georges Ernest Boulanger was at the height of his popularity in the 1880s. He attracted support for his triple program of revenge (on Germany), revision (of the Constitution), and restoration (of the monarchy). He was charged with treason, and was forced to flee the country, eventually committing suicide in 1891. Although Allais's political sentiments were usually private and often difficult to determine, he did seem sympathetic to Boulanger.

Although Jane Avril, also known as *La Mélinite* (or, to give her non-pseudonym, Jeanne Beaudon) is never mentioned in the following stories, her presence is certainly felt. A dancer at the Moulin Rouge, a tall thin redhead, she's best remembered today for the dashing figure she cut in Toulouse-Lautrec's posters and paintings. Allais was smitten with her around this time; he eventually proposed, and was refused. No doubt the many redheads in the stories here were inspired by her, and perhaps meant for her benefit.

I must advise the reader that "A Malcontent," originally intended as a monologue for Coquelin Cadet, is also included in the Black Scat edition of Allais's *Selected Plays*. As compensation, I've added four stories from the same period. The endnotes gloss the names, as I mentioned earlier, as well as topical allusions. The references are mostly incidental, and the stories are still funny without them, but Allais wrote firmly for his time and place, and the details are flavorful. I didn't gloss all of the locations in Paris, though; if you want to track the action, you can easily find a map. I also added the original dates of publication in *Le Chat Noir*. I couldn't trace four of the stories; they were either published elsewhere, or written especially for the book. Any information is welcome.

Allais went on to write hundreds more stories, collected in volumes that he called his "Anthumous Works," as well as a novel (*The Blaireau Affair*) and various plays, skits, and revues. Contemporaries noted that the strain of being funny all the time took its toll; alcohol and a bad marriage didn't help. He died in 1905, at the age of 51. Here, however, he's young and overflowing with invention, bent on giving Schopenhauer a hard time. Long live life, damn it!

Doug Skinner
New Paltz, NY
November, 2017

A NOTE TO THE READER

Apart from the pleasure I get by offending the spirit of Schopenhauer, I publish this volume for the sole objective of procuring myself a few resources.

I would therefore be grateful if The People not only bought *Long Live Life!*, but also recommended its acquisition to their friends and acquaintances.

THE AUTHOR

THE END OF A COLLECTION

You may recall the unfortunate experience of that collector of ma-
cabre, funereal, and criminal mementos, whose finest piece — the
detachable collar of a famous victim — was washed, starched, and
ironed by a maid who was zealous, but none too documentary.

A similar experience occurred, some twenty years ago, and even
a bit earlier, to an old gentleman I knew, named the Marquis de Bois-
Lamothe.

Quite a scamp in his day that marquis!

Rich, strong, handsome, a tireless skirt-chaser, unafraid of God
and friendly with the Devil, Bois-Lamothe was the terror of all the
husbands in the neighborhoods.

I say "neighborhoods," in the plural, because the marquis, a
great landowner as well as a frivolous and restless soul, changed his
neighborhood like his shirt.

Alas! We cannot both be and have been, as Francisque Sarcey, the
uncle of us all, has so wisely observed.

The Marquis of Bois-Lamothe had aged, his former girlfriends as
well.

From mortgages in licitation (?), the worldly goods of the marquis
had scattered to the four winds of the public auctions.

His coins had rung out so often that a cruel aphonia had ensued,
and had fallen so often that the most experienced eye could find no
trace of them, except of course in other purses.

Only one small patrimonial property had survived intact, too
intact even, since for twenty years, no gardener had spaded its soil, and
no woodcutter had attacked the proud upthrust of its heraldic oaks.

Disenchanted with everything, alone, the marquis discovered, one fine day, in his old withered heart, a fresh interest, a brand new interest that vibrated like a flourishing harp factory.

Bois-Lamothe had been taken by the mania, the rage, the delirium of collecting.

And what a collection!

The marquis collected shelled beans.

Those of my readers who have been to the country are familiar with beans (the others I don't write for. And let them remember it, once and for all).

Imagine 4,500 beans, of which the most similar still screamed — to the experienced eye — of disparatism.

There were white, black, blue, red, and violet. There were striped and spotted. There were yellow and violet, blue and orange, red and green.

They were no longer beans, they were polychromy fit for Antonin Proust to condemn.

This collection, which Bois-Lamothe knew by heart, every specimen, and which he loved like a second family, was completely contained within one huge bowl, full almost to overflowing.

And every morning, the marquis said to himself, in the language of the great past century: "And yet I should organize it! And yet I should organize it!"

But every evening settled upon the land, without it being organized, that precious collection.

❋

It was a radiant spring morning.

Bois-Lamothe had just gone out with his old dog and his old rifle to kill young rabbits.

Not long afterward, the rusty bell of the mansion produced sounds, muted sounds, already none too agreeable in themselves, but made even more inhospitable by the discourteous grinding of an oxidized curtain rod.

A sort of old servant, hideous, but extraordinarily dirty, and speaking French as if she had been raised in a boarding school for Spanish cattle, came to the door:

"What do you want?"

"Monsieur the Marquis de Bois-Lamothe."

"He's not here."

"Will he be back soon?"

"How should I know! Me, how should I know!"

Faced with this dubious welcome, the visitors decided to enter.

"I am Monsieur Bois-Lamothe's nephew," the man said, "and this is my wife. We will wait for my uncle in the house."

The walk, the open air, had probably given the visitors an appetite, for the young woman cried:

"What if we make lunch, while we wait?"

Consulted, the little old servant lifted her little old arms to the heavens, muttering her sempiternal: "How should I know! Me, how should I know!"

The marquis's niece then assumed an air of authority:

"Go find me some eggs! Wring a duck's neck! And be quick about it!"

Then, rummaging through the rooms, she discovered the famous bowl of beans.

Something happened then that is probably unique in the history of collections.

The young woman cooked the collection. When the collection was cooked, the young woman carefully drained it.

Then the young woman placed the collection into a pan with some butter and some thin slices of onion.

All at once, the old Bois-Lamothe manor smelled good.

The bright flame licked the pan, which sang of life, which sang of love, which sang of glory.

Just then the marquis returned.

You can imagine the cries of "Hello, uncle" that greeted the old gentleman.

The table was set.

They served a fine bacon omelet, and then a fine duck, and then...

And then...

And then... the beans!

Bois-Lamothe was not fooled for a second.

He recognized his white beans, his black, his blue, his red, his violet. He recognized his yellow and violet beans, his blue and orange, his red and green.

The marquis jolted to his feet, beat the air with his long thin arms, and collapsed backward onto an old Louis XIII clock, which had assuredly not marked twenty minutes since Henry IV.

He was dead.

Moral: Ridicule collectors all you like, but never make them eat their collections, even with onions.

CHIGNEUX

W hen, one beautiful morning — beautiful? — Monsieur the Baron Coudeuil de Travers was found murdered in his little wood the Bistoquettes, public opinion was unanimous in designating the guilty party as a certain Chigneux (Jules-César).

This Chigneux was a peasant, neither landowner, nor farmer, nor laborer, nor shopkeeper, nor industrialist, nor anything at all. He was accused of balancing his meager budget thanks to transfers favoring the vegetables of others, and his neighbors' hares, all simmered over dead — or green — wood that rarely carried a receipt.

Before the serious imputations of public opinion, Chigneux assumed an innocent air that changed all doubt to certitude, for as the eminent jurisconsult Bérard des Glajeux judiciously observed, whenever a defendant looks innocent, he's obviously guilty.

The brigadier of the gendarmerie launched an investigation that proved little, and a search that found nothing at all.

After having ransacked Chigneux's modest furnishings and uncomfortable bedding, the gendarmes were ready to leave, when their subject had the unhappy idea of lancing a final sally. Indicating his poor interior, devastated as if by an earthquake:

"And they claim," he laughed, "that you're representatives of order."

Chigneux had missed a fine occasion to keep quiet. Figuring that one joke deserved another, the brigadier returned and, striking with one hand a superb rabbit skin hanging from a joist and drying in the sun:

"How much did you pay for this at the market?"

This simple allusion to a minor hunting infraction defeated

Chigneux, whose physiognomy instantly took on an earthy color —
which, among unkempt countryfolk, is their way of turning pale.

Suddenly enlightened by Chigneux's pallor, the brigadier thrust an
inquiring hand into the rabbit skin. He brought out successively a wisp,
a portfolio containing several papers belonging to M. Coudeuil de
Travers, a wallet equipped with a hundred francs, and finally a watch
with the arms and initials of the late baron.

If you imagine that Chigneux was at all abashed by this extraction, I
pray you to scratch the notion from your tablets. Chigneux was simply
indignant.

"Ah! Good God dear God God damn it!" he cried. "If I knew that
scoundrel of a tramp who came here and stuffed all that in my rabbit
skin!"

In less time than it takes to write it, and without the slightest notice
taken of his rage, Chigneux was handcuffed and incarcerated in the
prison in Caen.

✻

At the preliminary hearing, Chigneux changed his tune.

He confessed, without confessing.

Well then! It was he who had killed the baron, but not to rob him,
good God! Chigneux was a poacher, and everything, but not a thief.

"And yet," objected the investigating judge, "the wallet? And the
watch?"

"Well then, exactly!" riposted Chigneux with brilliant presence of
mind. "That was to divert suspicion."

"???" marveled the magistrate.

"Well then, exactly! It was to suggest a robbery."

And Chigneux detailed with a thousand details an obscure and
touching love story. A young woman loved him whom he loved in
return. He was going to marry her, when the Baron Coudeuil arrived
and, by means of his gold, seduced the little one. So, heeding nothing

but his passion, Chigneux, one night, awaited the scoundrel. A blast from his rifle, bang, it was done! As for giving the name of the young lady, never on his life! Chigneux was a poacher, and everything, but not a slanderer.

This passionate crime version quickly caught on with the public. Every lady of Calvados worthy of the name took pity on Chigneux.

It was a fine trial.

Counselor Tocquard, one of the glories of the bar in Caen, achieved the unprecedented tour-de-force of surpassing himself:

"Gentlemen of the court, gentlemen of the jury, the man whom you have before your eyes is the most interesting personality I have ever had to defend in the already lengthy course of my noble career..."

And he told, poeticizing it, the tale of Chigneux, a delicious sylvan idyll.

Chigneux loved, he was loved. Soon, he would have lead to the altar, all pink under her white gown, the exquisite creature. Love would have restored this poacher to the veritable virginity of a gamekeeper. They would have been so happy. And then, a vile and debauched country squire poured torrents of despair and humiliation upon all this happiness... Ah, gentlemen of the jury!

Not very convinced, the gentlemen of the jury answered yes to some questions, no to others, and the court awarded twenty years of hard labor to our friend Chigneux.

At the indignant insistence of Counselor Tocquard, the conviction was overturned. One member of the jury, in fact, during the proceedings, had wished to one of his colleagues who had sneezed, that God bless him!

❅

Six months passed.

During this interval, water flowed under the bridge, Monsieur Grévy replaced Marshal MacMahon as President of the Republic, and

Counselor Tocquard, of the Caen Bar, a republican only the day before, was named district attorney to the court of Rouen.

It is precisely before this court of Rouen that the Chigneux affair was to unfurl anew.

On learning the name of the "public pretender," Chigneux emitted a cry of joy.

"The one who was my lawyer at Caen?"

"The same."

"Well then, now I'm happy. He's a pal, that guy!"

Counselor Tocquard arose to deliver his indictment.

"Gentlemen of the court, gentlemen of the jury, the man whom you have before your eyes..."

Chigneux was radiant. Obviously, Tocquard was going to repeat to the people of Rouen what he had said to the people of Caen.

"The man whom you have before your eyes," the prosecutor gravely repeated, "is the most dangerous character, the most fearsome brute I have ever been asked to contemplate in the course of my long career as a criminalist."

This time, Chigneux lost much of his confidence, in the proportions of 75 to 80 per cent.

The indictment continued in this rather malicious tone.

When Chigneux was asked if he had anything to add in his defense, he arose, and pointing to the prosecutor:

"I have only one thing to say, gentlemen," he declared, "and that is, as far as nerve goes, that man sure has a lot of nerve."

And he calmly sat down again.

The response of the jury was affirmative for all charges, mute on attenuating circumstances. The court, etc., etc., sentenced Chigneux (Jules-César) to death.

❋

Fortunately, we were living under a prince who opposed capital punishment.

Jules Grévy pardoned Jules Chigneux, who was, after a short delay, put on an ocean liner leaving for New Caledonia.

There, Chigneux was a "model prisoner." He was the object of various successive favors, and obtained a land grant.

Later, he married a charming young woman who had been sentenced to twenty years for throwing a newborn baby into the toilet — with the attenuating circumstance that she had closed the seat to protect the baby from the cold.

In short, Chigneux would now be the happiest of men, without the cruel burden of his contempt for the judges and lawyers of his beautiful homeland.

TOUSSAINT LATOQUADE

L ast week, I received an invitation conceived in these terms:

Monsieur and Madame Latoquade, annuitants of Port-au-Prince (Haiti), have the honor of inviting you to the marriage of Monsieur Toussaint Latoquade, their son, with Madame Cornélie Huss, née Pauss,
And ask you to, etc.

❉

Madame Cornélie Huss, née Pauss, widow, has the honor of inviting you to her marriage with Monsieur Toussaint Latoquade, student of medicine,
And asks you to, etc.

The first emotion that assailed me on reading this invitational prose was affliction: what, poor Huss was dead!

To tell the truth, the note made no mention of his demise; but my detective instincts were not fooled for a second, the state of widowhood in a woman being almost always determined by the death of her spouse.

When I had shed sufficient tears over the disappearance of the late Huss, I gave my soul over entirely to joy at the future union of his widow to my friend Toussaint.

Good old Toussaint!

To say that he was black would be an understatement. You would recognize him in shadows you could cut with a knife: he was blacker than the darkest night.

The chromotographers who maintain that absolute black cannot exist in nature are pathetic louts. If you don't know Toussaint Latoquade, hold your tongue. That's my opinion.

On arriving in Paris, he went to live in a furnished room on the place de la Sorbonne, where I myself stayed.

The building was managed by the Husses: Madame Cornélia Huss, a pleasant woman, coquettishly approaching thirty, and Monsieur Huss, a placid sort of character, but resolutely growing pale, through long nights, over the technical works of Jules Verne and Louis Figuier.

He could have, without affectation, put this placard on the door of his building: The concierge is an encyclopedist.

We often met, Toussaint and I, on the stairs. He offered a little smile, I a little nod; but, since we had no occasion to speak, we went no further.

One morning, one early morning, I heard a knock at my door.

"Come in," I grumbled from under the blankets.

(I always left the key in the door, in the hope that a dazzlingly beautiful and completely naked woman would enter my room, by mistake.)

It was Toussaint.

"Excuse me, my dear sir," he said, with the sweet melodious accent of his country, "I have a little Dutch canary who just escaped, and I think it's on your window."

"Take a look."

My window proved devoid of any canary, Dutch or otherwise.

The ice was broken; we met one another. The next time I saw him:

"And your Dutch canary?"

"Thank you, I found it."

Toussaint Latoquade quickly gained my esteem. He became my friend, and told me his story.

His parents had sent him to Paris to study medicine; but medicine bothered him, oh yes, it bothered him!

Besides, he failed his exams with a touching regularity that he never denied.

"It's that pig botany," he said angrily, "that I can't seem to get in my head!"

At other times, it was that pig anatomy, or that pig pathology.

I think he imagined the sciences as a herd of fierce, repellent, and malevolent swine.

Moreover, he was as lazy as a dormouse, and as good as the moon. He thoroughly belied his race's reputation for hard labor.

He was so good, poor Toussaint, and so innocent, that the entire Latin Quarter made him its plaything. And not just the white faces, but his most ebony companions. Everyone had fun with him.

Toussaint disliked student life, and gradually stopped frequenting the brasseries and tables d'hôte on the left bank.

He arranged with the concierges to have his meals with them. From then on, it was done: the Huss's apartment became his headquarters, and he never stepped more than thirty or forty meters from it.

At noon, he came down in his slippers (unforgettable slippers depicting a deck of cards), scarf, and flannel jacket, the whole topped with a white canvas cap, too small for his fine big frizzy head.

He ate leisurely, sipped endless mochas and liquors from all the islands, and smoked cigarettes, cigarettes, cigarettes.

(Have you ever seen a black man's fingers stained by cigarettes? Very curious.)

His belly full, he poked his nose out the door, and chatted with the coachmen at the station, all of whom knew him.

"Well, there's Monsieur Toussaint! How's it going, Monsieur Toussaint? A beautiful day! Will you stand me a drink?"

Toussaint responded that he was fine, that is was indeed a beautiful day, and that he would gladly stand him a drink.

One drink followed another, very gradually it became time for the vermouth, and then for dinner.

Dinner passed like lunch, the evening like the afternoon.

Thus were spent the days of Toussaint Latoquade.

From spending so much time in the Husses' apartment, he knew the tenants' addresses as well as they: Monsieur So-and-So, second floor on the left... Monsieur Whatsis, fifth floor, at the end of the corridor on the right.

It was a relief to the Husses, who could, from then on, enjoy a little recreation: Sunday in the country, sometimes the theater in the evening.

Toussaint, delighted to play a role in society, gave out information, and pulled the cord with the utmost grace.

At this point, my studies being completed (or at least they seemed so, to me), I left the Latin Quarter, and saw no more of my friend Toussaint, nor the Husses.

It took the marriage to remind me of them.

Naturally, I did not fail to attend the nuptial benediction. My word, it was very nice.

Madame Cornélie Huss, née Pauss, widow, as fresh as a rose, truly appetizing with her beautiful figure strapped into a pearl gray silk bodice, in the best of taste, and good old Toussaint, enormous in a frock coat less black than his loyal face, made a lovely couple.

At the sacristy, I congratulated them.

"Do you remember my Dutch canary that escaped onto your window?"

"Yes."

"It was a joke."

"How so?"

"Yes, it was a joke... I liked you a lot, and I thought up this way to meet you."

Good old Toussaint!

So, to amuse him, I said:

"Well, old man, the next time your Dutch canary comes to my

window and it's just a joke, send your wife after it! I'll give it to her right away."

I don't know exactly how Toussaint understood my apologue, but he received it with great hilarity.

SHOCKING

Before introducing you to the delectable Miss Sarah Vigott, allow me, as custom demands, to present her father and mother.

First, Monsieur Major Vigott.

Everyone calls him Major, without knowing exactly what he used to majorize. But what does the title matter, if the man is a gentleman, a true gentleman. And such is the case: Major Vigott is a gentleman in the full force of the term.

Physically, you must picture a little fat man, with a scarlet face, with short white muttonchops, with a big violet nose.

Violet is an understatement; we must, despite all the laws of grammar, call it "violets," so much did Major Vigott's nose display, according to the circumstances, different shades, oscillating between the most sumptuous burgundies and the most somber indigos.

His favorite drink was all fermented beverages and most known spirits.

Now, Madame the Majoress Vigott.

This person is not interesting enough to describe.

You've seen old Englishwomen, haven't you?

Well, Madame Vigott looks like all the old Englishwomen you ever saw. There, are you happy?

Madame Vigott's main characteristic is prudery.

To such an extent that she never allowed her cook to put a leek in the stew.

Now that you know the papa and mama, I will introduce you to Miss Sarah Vigott.

Blond, white, pink, sixteen, a cloud of mist!

This cloud of mist spent her leisure time in photography, and had attained a perfection in this art that would be the envy of the most accomplished professionals.

I forgot to tell you (but there's still time) that the Vigott family, like a host of other English families, had deserted the United Kingdom to make France its usual home.

The Vigotts live in a pretty little villa in Sainte-Adresse, with a view of the Baie de la Seine and that delicious coast that goes from Honfleur to Trouville.

✻

One day, Major Vigott (three weeks ago tomorrow), pleading urgent business in America, set sail, after a quick "goodbye" to his family, on the ocean liner *Champagne*.

The truth is that he was struck by the great beauty of a French actress, Madame Sarah Bernhardt, who was leaving for New York.

To travel with such a charming woman, O reverie!

I cannot claim that the French artiste spurned his advances, but the fact is that the very day after his arrival, the major boarded a steamer on the Cunard line, which took him back to Liverpool. Thirty-six hours later he was in Le Havre.

His short stay in America gave him enough time to purchase a marvelous instrument, the latest discovery of that inexhaustible inventor Blagsmith.

The "Telephotic," such was the name of the device. This instrument, an admirable combination of a telescope and an ordinary lens, permits photography of the most distant objects, as easily as if you had them at hand. It's wonderful!

I leave you to imagine the intense joy of the insubstantial Sarah Vigott when she unpacked the instrument. What beautiful snapshots she would take! The inventor of gelatin plates had suspended time, and now distance had become an empty word! Where will science end, my

God! And even, will it ever end!

Immediately, Sarah Vigott wanted to try her device (you know how girls are).

The weather was cold, but dry; the air was clear: excellent conditions.

Sarah turned toward the horizon the pale forget-me-nots that served her as eyes. With the help of the lens, she found, on the opposite shore, a delicious scene.

Beside the sea, a little meadow in which a conscientious painter strove to reproduce the beauty of winter. Beside the painter, seated on a folding chair, a young woman, probably his mistress (those people like nothing more than cohabitation), actively pursued a project of embroidery or knitting (I cannot confirm which).

Sarah focused the camera, inserted the plate, and click! pushed the trigger in question. That was it.

During the development of the picture, the Vigott family waited with bated breath, for they were vitally interested in Sarah's little projects.

This last finally emerged from the darkroom, holding between her rosy fingers the glistening plate of glass.

Everyone drew near.

※

Shakespeare alone (to this day!) could portray the horror of the scene.

Major Vigott let out more goddams in twenty seconds than are consummated in one year over the rest of the globe. His nose seemed successively illuminated by all the Bengal lights in the jubilee of the Empress of India.

Madame Vigott emitted a prolonged wail.

As for Sarah, she turned from pink to as red as a rooster dipped in a bucket of carmine.

Oh, those French artists!

Have you guessed what happened?

During the few seconds required for the insertion of the plate, after the lens was focused, the painter (for a landscape artist is still a man), arose, driven by an urgent need for effusion which you will excuse me from specifying.

He contributed, in his small way, to swelling the billows of the sea; the sea has seen worse.

It was Madame Vigott who first returned to a sense of reality.

Seizing the vile photograph with a pair of tongs, she flung it out the window.

Strange, strange: the next morning, the maid, sweeping the veranda, found not a single shard of glass.

Sarah Vigott had picked up the pieces.

In any case, now she only takes closeups.

STOPOVER ROMANCES

Captain MacNee, more generally known in the Scottish navy as Captain Steelcock, was what one might call a scoundrel. A charming scoundrel, but a thorough scoundrel.

His height was composed of six English feet and two inches of the same nationality, which equals, in our beloved metric system, two meters plus a few centimeters.

Quite elegant, as impassive as Lord Nelson's statue, loving women to the point of neglecting his most elementary duties, Steelcock was one of the few men in the Scottish navy to wear a monocle with such conviction. The men of the *Topsy-Turvy*, a pretty three-master where he was the commander, after God, even claimed that he slept with it.

Nobody, besides, in the *Topsy-Turvy* crew, could remember Steelcock ever taking part in anything resembling a command or maneuver.

Hands behind his back, always impeccably dressed, whatever the meteorological perturbations, he walked the deck of his ship with that detached and idle air that the gentlemen of Edinburgh assume on Prince Street.

Whenever his first mate, one of those old salts from Dundee, for whom the sea has no veil and the sky no mystery, communicated the "position," he tried to look prodigiously interested, but one could tell that his mind was distant, and that he didn't give a damn about whatever longitude or latitude they might cross.

Ah, yes! It was distant, that mind of his! Oh, how distant!

Steelcock was thinking about women, about women he had just left, about women he would see again, about women!

Sometimes he stayed for hours, leaning on the rail, contemplating the sea.

Was he expecting a mermaid to suddenly surface, or did he see in the rolling waves the cruel image of womankind? Are not the waves the perfect symbol — as poets have observed — of the foolish inconstancy and disturbing treachery of women? (Take that, ladies!)[1]

As soon as land was sighted, Steelcock stopped being a man, to become a cyclone of love, an apparently tranquil cyclone, but next to which the fiercest hurricanes were but gentle breezes.

Once the ship was in the dock, Steelcock sprinted ashore, leaving his old pirate of a first mate to deal with the customs and the shipbrokers, and he was off to town.

Do not believe in the slightest that the distinguished captain threw himself, like a rutting beast, on the first tempting flesh he saw, of which there is, alas! too much in our ports.

Oh, not at all! Steelcock loved women as women, but he also loved them for love, nothing seeming more delicious to him than to be loved exclusively, and for himself.

And what's more, with him, it never took long; he loved women so much that they had to love him too.

Affairs happened naturally with that tall and handsome lad. And besides, a properly worn monocle still enjoyed great prestige in the colonies and other analogous places.

One day, however, he was cured of his ridiculous mania for wanting (as if it were possible!) a woman to love him exclusively.

It was in Saint-Pierre (Martinique).

Steelcock had met the most delicious Creole you could imagine.

One would have to tear feathers from the Good Lord's angels and dip them in the blue of the heavens to write the charms of that woman. (The reader will understand if I abstain from this operation, which is

---

1. When the author wrote these lines, he thought his girlfriend was in the arms of another. At the present time (20 to 11) he is certain of the contrary. And so he retracts, with all his heart, the derogatory lines above.

both cruel and unavailable to me, at the moment).

In short, Steelcock came to know ecstasy, as if ecstasy and he had herded pigs together.

It's stupid, but that's how it is: moments of happiness pass more quickly than others (my God, how badly life is arranged!), the moment for departure arrived, and Steelcock could not bring himself to leave his beloved.

The *Topsy-Turvy* was in harbor, ready to sail, awaiting nothing but her captain.

Steelcock finally decided.

Loftily, he kissed the Creole and placed in her hand a certain number of pounds sterling, apologizing for his brutality, but having no time to find a more discreet present.

The young woman counted the gold pieces and put them in her pocket, with a rather disappointed air.

"Do you think," asked Steelcock, taken somewhat aback, "that the sum is insufficient?"

And the beloved replied, in that delicious twitter the women use as speech down there:

"Oh, no! You, you're very nice... it's your first mate who shortchanged me!"

This revelation was a blow to the captain's heart. A veil tore within him, and he saw how women were, after all.

From then on, he never sought exclusivity in love, contenting himself prudently with hygiene and comfort.

When he disembarked in different countries, he went straight to the professional lovers, as one goes to a grocer for jam and salt pork.

And he found himself none the worse for it.

Recently, he was obliged to land in one of the Lahila Isles (a Luxembourgian possession).

The Lahila Isles are famous throughout the Pacific, as much for the beauty of their climate as for the laxity of their morals.

A young lieutenant on the ship, Monsieur Julien Viaud, who later achieved a certain notoriety under the name of Pierre Loti, by writing exotic stories that are done quite nicely, I must say, composed the national hymn of this blessed country.

I can only recall the refrain:

Lahila Isles! Lahila Isles!
A very lovely place,
Lahila Isles! Lahila Isles!
To dock your keel awhiles.

Steelcock, barely ashore, asked for a good place.

He was politely directed to an avenue, behind the town, lined with elegant cottages whose inscriptions exuded welcome and understanding hospitality: Welcome House, Good Luck Home, Eden Villa, Pavillon Sans Fuss.

Steelcock had always had a weakness for the ladies of France. Therefore he resolutely entered the Pavillon Sans Fuss.

He was met by an old woman from Bordeaux, a bit shopworn, who introduced him to the residents.

Charming, the residents, and full of exuberance.

Steelcock fell under the spell of a little Toulonnaise, as black as jet, who could have done with a good combing, but nice all the same.

The lovers retired, and what they did during the night is nobody's business.

Early the next morning (you can check the papers for that day), an earthquake devastated the Lahila Isles.

The Pavillon Sans Fuss did not escape the disaster.

The ladies barely had time to escape in light, but professional, garments.

Only Steelcock and his companion missed the alarm.

The others were becoming seriously concerned about the unfortunate pair, when they saw approach, through a crack in the building, the captain, covered in plaster, but still impassive, his monocle in place.

"Say, madame," Steelcock cried to the woman from Bordeaux, "bring me another girl. Mine's dead!"

HISTORIA
SACERDOTIS BENE FINIS SECULI

The Marquise of Hautebeigne had been one of the prettiest women in the reign of Charles X, but the mounting financial woes, the accession of the cadet branch, the stupefying scandal of '48, the shameless outbursts of the Second Empire, the briberish nepotism of the Third Republic, the undeserved miseries of General Boulanger, all contributed forcefully to transforming the charming marquisette of earlier days into an old, pious, and charmless shrew.

Sequestered in her ancient castle in Hautebeigne, receiving nobody, except for the worthy Father Raoul, the marquise devoted herself, exclusively and without respite, to the salvation of her soul.

I have known many spiritual advisers, but I can affirm that I never met one fit to wipe the shoes of Father Raoul. A spirit advised by Father Raoul was a well advised spirit, a rare bird indeed in these times of shameful compromise and venal indulgence.

Although not a child, Father Raoul was still young; something around twenty-seven or twenty-eight.

Handsome, solidly stocky, gentle and humble in his manners, Father Raoul had no family name because, as it says in the song "The Family of Alphonse of Gros-Caillou," his mother had none either.

The circumstances attending the birth of this ecclesiastic are interesting enough for me to relate, without fear of boring the reader.

A farm servant, vigorous but clandestine, gave birth one fine day to a big baby boy, whom she placed, without delay, in a warm place: a pigpen.

Fortunately for the newborn, the residents happened to be staunch vegetarians, who showed, at the sight of their new little companion, understandable astonishment, but not the slightest inclination to consume him.

A few hours later, a villager, hearing the child's cries emanating from the pigpen, was struck with a horrible suspicion.

He was just in time: the baby was beginning to feel seriously inconvenienced by the ammoniacal vapors inherent in all good pig manure.

The young Moses, saved from the pigs, was entrusted to a nearby orphanage. As for his negligent mama, she was escorted in the direction of Nouméa, where she contracted, not long after, a brilliant marriage with a likable counterfeiter of those parts.

Raoul never ceased, for a minute, to edify the whole orphanage. He was still quite young when his calling became clear.

A kindly bishop even predicted an extraordinary future for him: the eminent prelate had no idea how right he was.

As soon as he was ordained, Father Raoul was named priest of the parish of Bitouilly, in which could be found the castle of Hautebeigne.

The marquise liked Raoul immediately.

His modest and pious air, his speech as unctuous as celestial cold cream, his horror of contemporary debauchery, went straight to the heart of the old woman, who deferred to him in all things, both divine and temporal.

The marquise had a little chambermaid, who was — and I fear no contradiction on this point — the prettiest young woman of the parish, and even the diocese.

Put the head of a young, impossibly blonde Englishwoman on the bust of a Burgundian wet-nurse — a virgin wet-nurse, of course — finish her off with the delicate extremities of the Duchess of X..., and you will obtain Sidonie.

Very modest, and rather ashamed of the copiousness of her figure, Sidonie concealed her indecent blouse under a sempiternal black cape that made her even more desirable.

But what did Sidonie care if her perishable flesh were desired? She strove to earn her place in paradise, her share, as they say in manille.

In short, you could hike a long time throughout the most pious countries in Christianity before meeting a trio as edifying as that of the noble marquise, the worthy priest, and the humble maid.

How different were the marquise's nephews! Oh how! The word "orgiastic" does not seem strong enough to vilify their usual conduct.

The youngest, especially, embodied a living scandal by parading throughout Paris as the official lover of the Calfskin Kid, and had already consumed, in similar sinful liaisons, two patrimonies and a future fortune.

The two other nephews were no better. My pen balks at the mere idea of tracing the graph of their excesses.

It was also a great sorrow for the poor woman, to think that her fortune, once she had departed, would help to swell the torrent of their filthy debauches.

Only once did she think they were returning to nobler sentiments. The three young men had attended high mass in the Bitouilly church, and sung the hymns with all the ardor of neophytes.

But when she learned, the next day, from Father Raoul, that the rascals had made a game of inserting

Impious words throughout the sacred text,

that was the last straw.

"Never," she cried, "will my fortune go to blasphemers!"

And, in defiance of feudal tradition, she disinherited her young relatives.

She had long discussions with Raoul about the proper allocation of her fortune.

The abbott gently dissuaded her from endowing a religious home. Doesn't the government stalk, like a famished wolf, religious treasure? When they claim rights to family estates, they are close to stealing them.

"But," cried Father Raoul as if suddenly inspired by the Holy Spirit, "do you not have at hand the best of legatees, she who, in short, will spend her life praying for the repose of your soul, she whose past promises a future of good works?"

"Sidonie, perhaps?"

"Herself."

The next day, a notary wrote a will making Sidonie the sole legatee of the Marquise de Hautebeigne.

It was just in time, for, a few days later, the old woman died.

I lack the space to describe the faces the nephews made when they heard the bad news, from the notary's mouth.

"What!" yelped the friend of the Calfskin Kid. "The old hag didn't leave us a pot to piss in!"

The honest notary probably thought it was a reference to a chamberpot, a souvenir of the late marquis, for he replied quietly:

"No, Monsieur Count, there is no mention of any pot in the will."

A few months elapsed after these events.

At this juncture, Father Raoul realized that his priestly calling had vanished from his heart.

He notified the bishop, threw his surplice on the scrapheap, and grew out his beard, which he then had barbered as elegantly as possible, into a point.

Then he married Sidonie.

GIOVENTÙ

To think that one was twenty, but is no more, and never will be again!

"Nevermore!" to quote Edgar Allan Poe, the American ancestor of our old friend Lucien Poe[1] (de Lapin), the well-known archeologist of the Butte.

And, speaking of the well-known archeologist of the Butte, let me offer you an anecdote that will give you an idea of Lucien's gift for repartee.

Gandillot, hoping to find a gift for a young woman who had granted him her ultimate favors, met Poe (de Lapin).

"Would you happen to have," asked the young and already famous dramatist, "some nice little plaster?"

"My poor Léon, I have no plaster, I'm just plastered."

But let us leave our dramaturgists and paleographers, and pick up the thread.

Twenty, I said; oh yes, twenty!

I don't know where you lived when you were twenty. Me, I stayed in a delicious little ground floor apartment situated on the sixth floor of a building on the boulevard Montparnasse, whose number I've forgotten (almost on the corner of the rue Vavin).

Very near my residence, the neighborhood housewives could procure the latest items at the Montparnasse Galleries.

I always wondered why the founder of that business put "galleries" in the plural. I don't even know why he would have put "gallery" in the singular.

---

1. Pronounced "Peau."

I never learned the reason, but that word "gallery" has always enjoyed the privilege of thoroughly astonishing me. A "gallery"!

The Montparnasse Galleries had nothing remarkable about them but their name and the manager's wife.

That last, at the present, assuming she is still alive, must no longer be in the first bloom of youth, for, at the time I'm talking about (oh, I was twenty!), she was already ripe; not enormously, but a little.

What did it matter? Her big black eyes, her Spanish kiss-curl, her little brown mustache, had all captured my poor heart, and I loved her, oh, I loved her!

At twenty, I was one of the stupidest boys of my age, as far as seduction was concerned (aside from that, remarkably intelligent).

I never dared declare my flame to Madame Gallery (that's what I called her, in my ignorance of any other designation).

Every morning, I met her doing her errands. I tipped my hat to her, with an expression that I tried to make indifferent.

She smiled at me very invitationally. And I ran away. What an idiot!

Regularly, every day, in the afternoon, I entered the store and made the purchase of a little four sou handkerchief (on sale at the end of the season, and never out of stock).

She accepted my twenty centimes with a smile that seemed like a glimpse of Eden, and I went away as red as the worst of roosters. My God, what a fool!

Aside from Madame Gallery, the personnel of the store consisted of Monsieur Gallery, a middle-aged man of doltish appearance, whose sole occupation was to season, on the doorstep of the building, meerschaum pipes of exceptional beauty.

In addition, three or four little salesgirls, rather homely, and a nondescript salesman.

One day — oh, the harrowing memory! — the nondescript salesman was replaced by a salesman as handsome as an engraving in the *Barbershop Gazette*, curled, pomaded, groomed — disgusting, in a word! I immediately vowed fierce hatred for this ignoble sub-salesclerk. My instincts had not failed me.

The very day that this individual entered the store, Madame Gallery stopped smiling at me as she did her errands. She accepted with an indifferent hand the four sous for my handkerchiefs (oh, those handkerchiefs! I think I still have some).

And me, I glared at the dandy with a look of defiance that seemed to astonish him.

Usually, I spoke, for the purchase of my handkerchiefs, to one of the salesgirls. One day, I spoke to the dandy, with the idea of giving him a hard time.

"Good day, sir," I said. "I would like a pocket handkerchief."

"Certainly, sir; just one?"

"Damn! I only have one nose, I only need one handkerchief."

"In cotton?"

"No... I don't pick cotton!"

The imbecile failed to understand all the subtlety of my joke. Finally, I indicated the famous four sou handkerchiefs.

"What initial, sir?"

"My name is Henri."

"Certainly."

And he brought me a handkerchief with an H in the corner.

"Excuse me, sir," I said, "but you're mistaken: it's written with an A."

"But no, sir, it's an H."

"I tell you it's an A! I should know, since it's my name."

"But I assure you, sir..."

"Stop bothering me and go back to school!"

I began shouting quite loudly. In exasperation, the salesman also started to yell a bit.

Monsieur Gallery, curious about the noise, stopped his seasoning for a moment and arrived.

"What's wrong?"

"What's wrong," I indignantly replied, "is that your imbecile of a clerk insists that Alphonse is written with an H... I know quite well, dammit, that there's an H in Alphonse, but not at the beginning of the word. Now, tell me if an initial (from the Latin *initium*) isn't the first letter of a word?"

Terrified by my shameless impudence, the dandy stammered vague explanations.

"But the gentleman told me his name was Henri."

"Henri! Is my name Henri? Do I look like my name is Henri? Why do you insist my name is Henri, when my name is Alphonse?"

My arguments appeared so conclusive to Monsieur Gallery that he, usually so calm, raised his voice:

"Write Alphonse with an H! We're not that stupid! Come now, you disgust me! You're leaving at the end of the month."

O triumph! My little joke had worked. My dangerous rival was out of the picture. Madame Gallery was mine!

(It goes without saying, he was much better than me, the rascal! Besides, I never claimed to be a pretty boy: women have always loved me for my intelligence.)

The end of the month arrived, and with it the departure of the handsome salesman. But, it was odd, I no longer saw my idol at the register.

The woman in the dairy next door solved the riddle for me:

"You don't know what happened at the Galleries?"

"No."

"Well, the manager fired his employee, and... his wife went with him."

This adventure cured me forever of mature women. Since then, I have only entrusted my heart to timid youngsters.

THE BIGHORNS

One fine morning, or rather one fine afternoon, it being an evening paper, the subscribers and purchasers of *l'Indépendant de Loing* could read, in that organ, the palpitating story that follows:

"The Scandal of the Café de la Poste. The little town of Toutaleuil, usually so peaceful, was awakened last night, around eleven thirty, by an inexpressible commotion that seemed to come from inside the Café de la Poste.

"This establishment, managed by Monsieur Tâtort (Victor), has always been considered the most peaceful and respectable cafe in Toutaleuil, and there was legitimate astonishment at the unusual noise it produced at such an advanced hour of the night.

"Immediately notified, the captain of the police donned his scarf and went to knock at the door of the criminal establishment, ordering the manager to open, in the name of the law.

"The official received no answer to his order but a redoubling of the noise, produced by the shattering of tables, glasses, saucers, bottles, and in general all of the objects that combine to form the equipment of a bar.

"He resorted to drastic measures, and a locksmith, a certain Sarcey, opened the door of the Café de la Poste.

"The witnesses were then able to witness an inexpressible and deplorable scene.

"Two honorable citizens of Toutaleuil, the Messieurs O. de la Dhuys, retired colonel of the hussars, and Leroy-Datout, former merchant, had come to blows, emitting nameless roars, foaming at the mouth, stamping the floor with their feet, and launching in reciprocal directions any object at hand.

"At her register, terrified, white-faced, Madame Tâtort, who seemed to understand nothing of the scene, was principally occupied in shielding herself from the debris of this unspeakable battle.

"In the back, in the kitchen, one could see the manager of the establishment, Monsieur Tâtort, whose defeated and haggard face was painful to see. The poor man had taken refuge in a corner, and seemed eager for an end to the scandal.

"The police captain, assisted by two deputies, tried to get between the two combatants. But these last, whose fury multiplied their strength, made short work of the functionaries, and soon tossed them a considerable distance away.

"All intervention was then abandoned.

"The struggle soon ended.

"Monsieur Leroy-Datout threw himself, head lowered, with exceptional violence, at the colonel's stomach.

"The former superior officer collapsed and fell onto a heap of broken glass, which cut him rather badly.

"To the great astonishment of the witnesses, Monsieur Leroy-Datout rushed toward, even pounced upon, Madame Tâtort, and, enfolding her in his arms, carried her off, disappearing through the door that had unwisely been left ajar.

"A few minutes later, he had disappeared into the night.

"As for the colonel, he vehemently refused all medical attention, and, in the middle of his bellowing, one could make out these words:

"'I'll find him, that filthy civilian bighorn!'

"These incomprehensible words lead us to attribute the regrettable incident to a double case of spontaneous insanity.

"By the time we went to press, Monsieur Leroy-Datout and Madame Tâtort had not yet been found.

"They are thought to be hiding in the forest of Saint-Polyte.

"We shall return, in our next issue, to this curious affair."

※

Monsieur Oscar de la Dhuys and Hector Leroy-Datout were very close.

Habits of long standing brought them together at the Café de la Poste, the former colonel and the retired merchant, where they indulged in the simple pleasures of piquet and dominos.

They also read the Paris papers, alternately, each passing a sheet to the other after he had read it.

Often they called their mutual attention to such and such an article in such and such a paper.

So it was, that one day the colonel strongly recommended to the former merchant an article concerning the discoveries — then recent — of Dr. Brown-Séquard.

"And yet! What if it were true!"

And there they were lost in a dream, the poor old duffers.

For it was not only from business that he had retired, Monsieur Leroy-Datout; and as for the colonel, it was not only as a servant of Mars that he had decamped.

But, as the song says, one is always twenty in some corner of the heart. For them, it was in every corner of the heart that they were twenty. And only in the heart, alas!

Each of them embodied a brilliant past of love and sensuality.

The colonel, he had broken hearts by the millions. So many hearts, and so many hearts, that his hammer was worn out.

And then it seemed to him — a senile illusion — that the hearts of today were harder than they used to be. The old fool!

As for Monsieur Leroy-Datout, he never had a reputation as a woman chaser, because his profession enabled him to have at hand everything needed for love.

He adored redheads, and, in the vast workshops and storerooms of the rue du Sentier, there never appeared the tiniest blonde or brunette employee. All fire-colored.

That led to some strange incidents.

When these demoiselles appeared at the window together, uninformed passersby had at first the illusion of a terrible fire, and it was only after closer inspection that the gentlemen realized their error.

And even, one day, a zealous passerby ran to alert the firemen of the rue Jean-Jacques-Rousseau. The modest heroes arrived in great haste in their melodious wagon.

Attracted by the noise, the demoiselles of the Leroy-Datout emporium had no more urgent need than to rush back to the window.

As it happened, they were myopic firemen, who, victims of their error, thoroughly drenched the fulgurous females.

※

"And what if it were true, that invention of Brown-Séquard's!"

And they started to contemplate, with God knows what gleams in their pupils, the beautiful wife of the manager, enthroned at her register, superb, very brunette, a bit ripe, but devilishly appetizing, and those eyes!

"And yet, what if it were true!"

And they chatted about other things, distractedly. Deep inside, they were thinking it was funny that one could, with an injection from a guinea pig, rabbit, or dog, regain the supreme joy of *potency*.

A few days later, the colonel recommended that the merchant read one of those little features in *La France,* in which Papa Fulbert-Dumonteil parades the habits of all the animals, from the sole au gratin to the Panther of Batignolles.

This time, it concerned the bighorn, an animal dear to Bergerat.

"...His loves are ardent and jealous, almost as formidable as his rages. When comes the spring, the bighorn collects himself a harem amid the green myrtle and pink heather, and woe betide any audacious rival who dares approach! Among bighorns, war is always mixed with love, and these are homeric combats, terrifying battles. The earth rings hollowly under the rivals' hooves, and one can hear from afar the clatter of horns that puts to flight both eagles and vultures (sic).

"Sometimes, the strength and hatred are equal; the struggle remains uncertain, the victory indecisive. The bighorns, exhausted by fatigue and rage, reluctantly abandon the battlefield and the love that they have soaked with their blood. But it is only postponed; as they disappear behind the rocks, they stop and threaten one another with their horns, stamping upon the ground, and seeming to say, 'We will meet again next spring! *Sangue et vendetta!*'"

"Well," concluded the colonel, "what lovers!"

Monsieur Leroy-Datout had an idea.

"What if Brown-Séquard used a bighorn for his injections?"

"That might be amusing."

❈

In the course of the following week, the Toutaleuil fair opened.

One of the most popular attractions of the fair, the Corsican Menagerie, presented by a certain Cappaza, had a bighorn.

The same idea occurred to the colonel and the merchant, who made a serious mistake by hiding it from one another.

The clever animal trainer reaped twice the profit.

The pharmacist in Toutaleuil (a laureate of the Pharmaceutical College of Paris) prepared, with a discretion fully equal to his fee, the mixture conforming to Brown-Séquard's latest instructions.

Unfortunately, fate demanded that the two gentlemen use it the same day.

SUPPLY TRAIN

I t is considered good taste in the French army to mock the supply train. Quite impervious to these taunts, the good soldiers ignore them, knowing full well, in short, that only in the supply train does everyone have horses and carriages.

Horses and carriages! That horizon convinced the young Gaston de Puyrâleux to enlist in the force, which he considered elite, for a term of five years.

Before coming to this decision, Gaston had thought it best to devour two or three inheritances in the time that it takes the Sahara to absorb, at the stroke of half past noon, the contents of a miniature watering can.

Gambling, investment tips, women, small parties, and large parties had plucked the young Puyrâleux to the marrow. Nevertheless, it was cheerfully and without regrets that he "joined" the 112th regiment of the supply train in Vernon.

An optimistic philosopher, this Gaston, with the motto: "Life is what you make it."

And he set out to make his life amusing, amusing without respite, amusing anyway.

In love with carriages, crazy about horses, no credit can be given Puyrâleux for becoming the cream of the service force.

His proverbial skill was soon the stuff of legend: he could drive the most copious convoy through the eye of a needle without touching either side.

※

Vernon is surrounded by charming country, but personally is a rather disagreeable seaport. To cite but one detail, it lacks women, and how! Women worthy of the name, do you understand?

Between low debauchery and adultery, Gaston de Puyrâleux didn't hesitate a second: he chose both.

He loved successively dealers in commercial love and sentimental butchers' wives, all without neglecting two or three officials' wives and a Fat Lady in the sideshow.

Let us add that this last passion remained platonic, and proved disastrous to the career of the young and brilliant officer of the supply train.

Was the Belle of the Ardennes really the most beautiful woman of the century, as it said on the sign to her booth? I cannot confirm it, but she was certainly one of the most voluminous...

Her calf could have served as a thigh to more than one beauty; as for her thigh, only a surveyor's chain could have assessed its suggestive contours.

Her outfit was composed of a dress of copper plush, which harmonized divinely with a toque of scarlet velvet. Exquisite, I tell you.

And thus it was that this idiot Gaston came to fall in love, fiercely in love, with the Belle of the Ardennes!

But the Belle of the Ardennes did not weigh so many kilos to become a woman of light morals, and Puyrâleux had no success with his amorous expenditures and the effect of his best dress dolman.

You do not know Puyrâleux if you think him capable of accepting such a humiliating defeat.

He assured himself that the Belle of the Ardennes spent the night alone in her trailer, the showman and his wife sleeping in another wagon.

Gaston's plan was of Biblical simplicity.

❈

One dark night, assisted by Plumard, his faithful orderly, he arrived at the fairground, which was troubled only by the faint cries of melancholy animals.

In less time than it takes to write it, he hitched two government horses to the Fat Lady's trailer, released the wheels, kicked out the blocks...

And there they were speeding off toward the sleeping countryside.

At first there was no sign, in the car, of the presence of a living soul.

But soon, once past the last houses, a window opened to give passage to a loud harsh voice, used to brief commands, which emitted a formidable "Halt!"

The good horses dutifully stopped, and Puyrâleux disguised himself immediately as a supply train officer who was not very happy.

The loud harsh voice came from a throat well known in Vernon, the throat of Major Baron Leboult de Montmachin.

Having accepted the situation, Puyrâleux approached the window, his kepi in hand.

By the pale light of the stars, the major recognized the corporal.

"Ah, it's you, Puyrâleux?"

"My God! Yes, Major."

"What the hell are you doing here?"

"My God, Major! Let me tell you: since I had a bit of a headache, I thought a little trip in the country..."

During this conversation, somewhat painful on both sides, the major adjusted his uniform, which was not impeccable at the time.

The Belle of the Ardennes greeted Gaston with remarks full of discourteous vulgarity.

"You will do me the kindness, Puyrâleux," concluded Major Leboult de Montmachin, "to drive this car back to where you took it... We will discuss this particular matter tomorrow morning."

It is useless to add that the two gentlemen never spoke about the particular matter, but Puyrâleaux was not surprised, at the end of class, to see that he had not been promoted to sergeant.

And he regretted it keenly, for he enjoyed serving in the supply train, and had hoped to make an honorable career of it.

THE SPRINKLER

I t was spring!

A spring that bloomed late, but soon became radiant, and perhaps even torrid.

Young ladies at last unmittened — at last! — pattered along briskly, pretty as pictures, in their bright dresses and hats, hats with fading tender blue ribbons or pink feathers, so lightly pink that they looked like feathers torn from the wings of the soul. It was spring!

With their tables and chairs, barkeeps encumbered the surrounding asphalt, leaving nothing for the passage of pedestrians but the insufficient and granitic edge of the sidewalk. It was spring!

The ladies of the middle classes examined their husband's alpaca of yore, and, not without joy, confirmed that it would still be quite serviceable this year. It was spring!

In the left bank cafes, tumultuously coiffed young men demanded "something to write with," and, in clipped but vigorous verses, proclaimed the Glory of the Earth's Awakening. It was spring!

The oxygen and nitrogen in the air had politely given way to the volatilized aroma of so many lilacs, and everywhere, in the leafage, buds popped open like rude little boys. It was spring!

Joy was painted on all faces, except one.

Except one: that of a fine young man, whose name was, and still is, for that matter, Gaston de Puyrâleux.[1]

Recently liberated from military service, Gaston had had just

---

1. I request the ladies and gentlemen reading this, if it's not too much trouble, to consult the preceding story.

enough time to devour an inheritance from his uncle, who deserves a short mention in passing.

The old Duke Loys de Puyrâleux, after an existence of unalloyed austerity and agronomy, fell, in the course of one of his trips to Paris, into the charming trap laid by a young woman devoid of etiquette known as the Washroom Kid. One night, the poor apoplectic gentleman expired in the arms of this raspy siren, on the fourth floor of an apartment house on the rue Lamarck (eighteenth arrondissement).

Very fin-de-siècle, Gaston gave a generous present to the Washroom Kid, organized a decent funeral for his Uncle Loys, and knew no rest until his little fortune had passed into other hands, half hookers, half card sharks.

"When I run out of money," he said with the philosophy of a man of twenty-five, "I'll blow my brains out."

The time came, more punctually than it should have, and his brains were not blown out.

Does one blow out one's brains in weather like that? (For I believe I have already mentioned above that it was spring.)

Gaston de Puyrâleux had reached that point in his reflections, when he met on the boulevard a fat man he had known in Tréport.

"Well, Monsieur de Puyrâleux!... How are you?"

"Very well, thank you... That is, when I say very well, you know..."

"Are you ill?"

"No, but..."

And Gaston narrated his sad situation to the fat man.

The fat man happened to be, a detail unknown to Gaston, a successful contractor for street cleaning in the City of Paris. He sympathized keenly with the young man's distress.

"If I dared offer you a place in the office?"

"Oh, office work! You know, I'm not too good at that."

"But I couldn't suggest that you drive a sprinkler truck."

"Why not?"

"What? You'd consent to..."

"Absolutely!... Me, as long as I have my butt in a seat and some reins in my hand, that's all I need."

"!!!"

"As far as competence is concerned, you can depend on me. I just left the supply train, and I could drive an artillery wagon from Paris to Orléans on a telegraph wire."

"It's agreed, then."

"Agreed."

And the next morning, the last of the Puyrâleux set out to sprinkle copiously the Place de la Concorde, which had been assigned to him.

It was spring!

Young ladies at last unmittened — at last!... *(See above.)*

It was so thoroughly spring that Gaston completely lost his exact notion of things.

Carriages streamed into the Park.

Gaston, a chestnut flower in his buttonhole, thought himself still in his age of glory.

He sent his valiant steed a crack of the whip, and headed down the avenue des Champs-Elysées. (Have you ever noticed that in stories steeds are always valiant steeds?)

Now, he trotted gaily along, paying no attention to the water cascading behind him.

All of his old friends, all of his former girlfriends recognized him with alarm. He waved at them graciously: Hello, old fellow! Hello, dear! Greetings, you old fool!

Truth compels me to admit that his advances were greeted more coldly.

The barrel emptied out on everyone, on the legs of horses, on the wheels of carriages. A family out for a drive in a low cart was completely inundated.

Thus did Gaston arrive at the lake in the park.

The presence of a sprinkler truck trotting among the elegant carriagework caused an abominable scandal.

A park guard intervened, and confided Gaston and his hydraulic device to two policemen, who conducted the whole thing to the pound.

The young count took it all cheerfully, but all of the old Puyrâleux, from those in Azincourt to the one on the rue Lamarck, within their quiet graves, were trembling with despair (my word, that's a fine alexandrine!): for the first time, one of their own and his equipage had been taken to the pound.

It was spring!

THE HOMICIDAL AUTOGRAPH

had been away from Paris for several months, very busy with an exploratory voyage into the northwest region of Courbevoie.

When I returned to Paris, letters had accumulated on my office desk; among them, one bordered in black.

Thus it was that I had the sad surprise of learning of the death of my poor friend Bonaventure Desmachins, deceased in his twenty-eighth year.

"What?" I cried. "Desmachins! A lad so healthy, of such a vigorous constitution!"

But when I learned, a few hours later, how Desmachins had died, my sad surprise gave way to such keen astonishment that I was floored (oak).

"What?" I repeated. "Desmachins! A lad so tidy, so virtuous!"

The fact is that the thing seemed unlikely.

Poor Desmachins! I can still see him so calm, so well combed, so well ordered in his existence.

He had his little obsessions, my God! But who doesn't?

For example, he would not have, not for a cannonball, bought a postage stamp anywhere than from the tobacconist in the Théâtre-Français. He claimed that by patronizing this shop, he saved a great deal of money, the tobacconist's stamps being dryer, and consequently lighter and less likely to overload his correspondence.

An innocent obsession, don't you think?

If this were Desmachins's only little weakness, he would still be alive today. Unfortunately, he had a passion that was apparently undangerous, but which, nevertheless, led him to his grave.

Desmachins collected autographs.

He collected them as a lioness loves her cubs, fiercely.

And did he have autographs! Did he! My God, did he!

Of everyone, for example: of Napoleon I, of Yvette Guilbert, of Chincholle, of Henry Gauthier-Villars, of Charlemagne...

It's true that the Charlemagne!... I knew its provenance, but, to avoid upsetting Desmachins, I always kept, about that falsely aged parchment, a golden silence.

(It was an old student of the Library School, fallen into a life of crapulous improbity, who had taken up the fabrication of Carolingian — do not write Carnalingian — manuscripts, and who furnished Desmachins with autographs from the most distant antiquity.)

The friend who had informed me of Desmachins's demise, in all its painful detail, seemed to struggle with a desire for confession.

Finally, he murmured:

"And what is the most terrible, is that I am in a way his murderer."

At that, my sad surprise was colored by astonishment.

"Yes," he continued, "poor Desmachins died from my advice."

"Guillotined by persuasion, I suppose!"

"Oh, don't laugh! It's an appalling story, and I'll tell it to you."

I assumed the well-known attitude of a gentleman about to be told an appalling story, and my friend — for, in spite of everything, he's still my friend — narrated the thing to me in these terms:

One day, I met Desmachins delighted with a new acquisition. He had just bought a mutton bone on which was inscribed, in the hand of the Prophet himself, a verse of the Koran.

"And you paid how much...?" I asked.

"A crust of bread, old man. It was an old Arab sheik who sold it to me. Since he was desperately in need of money, I was able to get the object for 3000 francs."

"Damn!" I thought. "A crust of bread! That makes a lot per pound."

And he took me to his house to admire his new filing system. He had, he told me, invented a new filing system of which he was very proud.

The sight of a letter from Nélaton suggested an idea to me, and, without thinking, I asked:

"You don't have Ricord's autograph?"

"Ricord?... Who's that?"

"What? You don't know Ricord?"

The unfortunate man... that is to say, the fortunate man... or rather, no, the unfortunate man didn't know Ricord.

And so, me, I sang the praises of Ricord, and Desmachins at once swore to obtain, for his collection, a note from the celebrated specialist.

The very next day, he visited his usual dealers: not the smallest "Ricord."

At his unusual dealers, nothing either.

Desmachins was disappointed and impatient. For he, habitually so calm, changed easily into a wild beast, where his collection was concerned.

"And yet," he roared, "there are people who have his autograph!"

"Yes," I gently replied, "but those who own them are more likely to bury them in the most intimate folds of their portfolios, rather than draw some frivolous vanity from them."

"That gives me an idea! Since Ricord is a doctor, I'll go visit him, he'll write me a prescription that he'll sign, and I'll have the autograph."

"That's ingenious, but unfortunately... or rather, fortunately, you're not ill."

"I have a bad head cold... See, my nose is running."

"Your nose..."

I went no further, having always had a horror of tasteless jokes, but I enlightened Desmachins on the role that Ricord played in contemporary society.

Eight days passed.

One morning, Desmachins visited me, pale, but with determination in his eyes.

"You know, I've decided!"

"About what?"

"To go to Ricord."

"But, once again, you're not... ill."

"I will be!... And in fact I've come to ask you for details."

I thought he was joking, but not at all! It was an obsession.

So — and it will be the eternal regret of my life — I had the weakness to furnish him with a few explanations. I suggested the Folies-Bergère, from personal experience.

The following week, Desmachins sent me a telegram, which read:

"Come see me. I'm in bed. But so what! I HAVE IT."

The last three words triumphantly underlined.

"Yes," the narrator sadly concluded, "he had it, and that's what killed him."

CORYDOR

His godfather, a fanatic tree surgeon from Meaux, had insisted that he be named, like himself, Polydore. But we, his friends, quite rightly considering the name Polydore supremely ridiculous, had quickly saddled the fine lad with the sobriquet "Corydor," much prettier, and more euphonic and suggestive.

He, besides, was delighted with the name, and his calling cards bore no other. In addition, one could read in handsome gothic letters "Corydor," on the copper plaque adorning the door of his little ground floor apartment, situated on the sixth floor of 327 rue de la Source (Auteil).

He insisted only that his name be spelled as I have given it: one R, and with Y rather than I.

Let us respect this inoffensive obsession.

I have not attained my current age without seeing many unusual specimens, but the most unusual specimens I have had to contemplate seem like pale little whatsits next to Corydor.

Someone, Victor Hugo, I think, called Corydor the likable head of the Screwball school, and he was absolutely right.

Every time I see Corydor, my whole being shivers with delight down to its most intimate fibers.

"Good," I say to myself, "here's Corydor, I won't be bored."

A prognosis that has never disappointed.

Yesterday, I received a visit from Corydor.

"Take a good look at me," said my friend. "Do you see a change in my face?"

I contemplated Corydor's features, and nothing special appeared to me.

"Well then, old man," he replied, "you're not much of a physiognomist. I'm married."

"Oh, bah!"

"Yes, my good fellow. Married for a week... A thousand more to wait and I'll be a happy man!"

"A thousand what?"

"A thousand weeks, by God!"

"A thousand weeks? Waiting for what?"

"When I've lost two hours telling you about it, you still won't understand!"

"So you think I'm stupid?"

"It's not that you're stupider than the next man, but it's such a funny story!"

And on that tantalization, Corydor draped himself in a sepulchral silence. I would risk anything, even crime, to know the rest.

"So," I said in my most indifferent tone, "you're married..."

"Absolutely."

"Is she pretty?"

"Ridiculous."

"Rich?"

"Not a sou."

"Then what?"

"Because I tell you that you won't understand."

My pleading eyes made him reconsider.

Corydor settled into an armchair, did not light an excellent cigar, and narrated what follows:

"Do you remember the vile weather that the Good Lord lavished upon us throughout the pretty month of May? I took advantage of it to leave Paris, and went to Trouville to yield my alabaster body to the kisses of Amphitrite.

"In that season, in Trouville, apartments are nothing. For a mere crust of bread, I rented an entire house, on the road to Honfleur.

"Ah, it was such a funny house, my poor friend! Imagine a happy mixture of Florentine palace and Norman cottage, with a hint of Hindu pagoda over everything.

"Between two of Amphitrite's kisses, I made vague excursions into the surrounding area.

"One Sunday among others — oh, that unforgettable Sunday! — I was walking through Houlbec, a pretty little seaport, I must say, when I was suddenly drenched with torrents of harmony.

"A few steps away, on a plaza planted with centenarian elms, a brass band, probably municipal, hurled its most melodious bellows to the heavens.

"And around them, all around those enraptured Orpheuses, ceaselessly turned the Houlbecqois and Houlbecqouises.

"Among the latter...

"Do you believe in love at first sight? No? Well, you're an absolute moron!

"Me neither, I didn't believe in love at first sight, but now!...

"It's like something hits you, bang! right in the pit of the stomach, and then spreads a bit through your whole belly. Very curious, love at first sight!

"Among the latter, as I was saying, a tall brunette, about forty, was turning, turning, turning.

"Was she pretty? I have no idea, but when I saw her, I knew at once that she was made for me. I loved that woman, and will never love anyone but her.

"Mock me if you will, but that's how it is.

"She was accompanied by her daughter, a hideous tall maiden of twenty, graceless and angular.

"The next day, I had abandoned Trouville, and my Auvergno-

Japanese castle, and installed myself in Houlbec.

"My love at first sight was the wife of a captain in the customs, an old fellow who was gruff as anything, and a player of auction manille, as fervent as the late Manille himself at an auction.

"I, who had never learned to hold a card in my life, did not hesitate, to draw nearer to my idol, to become the partner of that terrible tax collector!

"Oh, those evenings at the Café de Paris, those atrocious evenings consecrated solely to the captain calling me an imbecile, because I had trumped his hand, or hadn't trumped it. Because, to this day, I still don't really know.

"And besides, I could never remember that it's the ten that's highest in that game. Oh, my head, my poor head!

"Finally, one day, after about a week, my constancy was rewarded. The tax collector invited me to dinner.

"Charming, the captainess, and an exquisite hostess. My heart burned like a smoldering ember. I put everything in motion to achieve my detestable ends, but I failed in every sense of the word.

"I was beginning to feel thoroughly calamitous, when one evening — oh, that unforgettable evening!... We were in the salon: I was leafing through an album of photographs, and she, my idol, was identifying: My cousin Such-and-such, My aunt What's-her-name, my husband's sister-in-law, my uncle So-and-so, etc., etc.

"And that one, do you recognize her?"

"Perfectly, that's Mademoiselle Claire."

"Oh no, not at all! That's me at twenty."

"And she told me that when she was twenty, she looked exactly like Claire, her daughter, so exactly that when she looked at Claire it was like looking in the mirror twenty years ago.

"Was it possible!

"How could that adorable creature, so deliciously plump, have been such a thin and bony girl?

"So, my poor friend, an idea occurred to me that inundated me with light and joy.

"At last, happiness was at hand!

"If the mother resembled the daughter so exactly, I said to myself, certainly one day the daughter will resemble the mother exactly.

"And that's why I married Claire, last week.

"Today, she's twenty, and she's ugly. But in twenty years, she'll be forty, and she'll be as radiant as her mother.

"I'm waiting, that's all"

And Corydor, obviously very proud of his plan, added:

"You won't be calling me crazy now, eh?"

LIGHTHOUSES

Eure is probably one of the few landlocked departments in France, and certainly the only one to possess a maritime lighthouse.

Following what shady intrigues, what base maneuvers, what nauseating influence did this freshwater department manage to have a first-class lighthouse built in its heart? That is something I cannot say, something I never wish to know.

A few youngsters in the Department of Civil Engineering will answer smugly that a lighthouse raised on solid ground can light a portion of the sea lying not too far away. So be it!

It makes it no less humiliating, when one lives in Honfleur (settlers from Honfleur founded Quebec in 1608), and a friend, O'Reilly or another, asks you to take him to a first-class lighthouse, it makes it no less humiliating, I say, to drag him into a neighboring department whose most intrepid navigator is a tanner in Pont-Audemer.

Not that the voyage is regrettable, oh, certainly not! The road is charming from one end to the other, peopled with old sempiternals at their knitting, and young women waiting at the fountain for their buckets to fill. Ah, how exquisite they are, those Norman danaids, one especially,[1] just before Ficquefleur!

So, we arrive in Fatouville: there's the lighthouse.

A guard welcomes you, he's the head guard, don't forget, a first-class head guard, as he is careful to notify you himself.

We climb a staircase that contains a certain number of steps (without them would it be a staircase? has so justly observed that cruel observer Henry Somm).

---

1. I have since learned that this particular Norman danaid was born on the rue des Dames (Batignolles), but it makes no difference, I love her anyway.

Those steps, I knew how many there were yesterday, but I don't today. Forgetfulness, that's life.

When we reach the top, we enjoy a superb view, as people say. We discover (I had again forgotten this quantum) a considerable amount of square miles of territory. Why square miles in a circular panorama?

"What is that little lighthouse?" asks one of our companions, indicating a point on the Lower Seine.

"A lighthouse, that? You call that a lighthouse?" the guard replies, vaguely indignant.

Our companion, embarrassed, is suffused with them (blushes).

"That's not a lighthouse, madame, it's a fire."

He even tells us the name of the fire, but I forgot it like everything else.

When we had discovered enough territory, we descended the number of steps that constitute the staircase that I mentioned earlier.

A guestbook holds out its arms to us, so that we might trace within it our visitors' names.

I modestly sign Francisque Sarcey, adding in the space for "Observations" this ingenious phrase:

.   .   .   .

The phrase that I inscribed has escaped my memory, like so many other stories.

I leaf through the guestbook, and cannot believe the stupidity of my contemporaries.

What idiots people are, my God! What idiots!

The "Observations" section of the Fatouville guestbook certainly constitutes one of the finest monuments to human stupidity that one might contemplate upon the face of the earth.

A whole firmament of moons would give but a feeble idea of it.

I except a quatrain that is a few months old, by Georges Lorin, and a reflection from Pierre Delcourt.

Lorin's quatrain boasts a hair-trigger mechanism; as for Delcourt's sentence, it alone repels all boarders.

Here is the quatrain:

A woman's beauty drives
The puns a husband craves:
A beacon brightens waves,
A beckon brightens wives.

And now for Delcourt:

The Fatouville lighthouse is nothing, after all, but a gigantic candle. It has, in the same proportions, the same form and illuminating power.

Then we withdrew.

We were about to get into our car, when a sort of funny little man, not very old, but not extraordinarily young either, extremely gaunt, asked us politely if we were returning to Honfleur. On our assurance that it was indeed our goal, the funny little man asked for a small place in our vehicle, to which we consented with the best grace in the world.

En route, he confessed that he was an inventor, and that he was going to revolutionize the entire administration of lighthouses.

"Are you interested in lighthouses, gentlemen?" he asked.

"Oh, you know, we're interested without being interested."

"You're mistaken, for it's a fascinating question."

I had a strong urge to ask the inventor to procure us a little silence. We drove along the coast, through a magnificent countryside upon which a clement October tossed her discreet gold. I felt more inclined to enjoy the view than to hear the old duffer's ravings. But the old duffer continued, aflame with ardor:

"Lighthouses, they're okay when the weather is clear; but is the weather ever clear?"

"Well, I've sometimes seen..."

"The weather is never clear! So..."

"We have the foghorn that bellows in the mist."

"The foghorn is a joke. I defy any navigator sailing in the fog to tell me, within 30 degrees, the direction of a foghorn, if it's a few miles away. So, I invented something else. Because you can't see the light of the lighthouse, and you can't tell the direction of the sound of the foghorn, I created the odoriferous lighthouse. Listen to this."

"Go to it!"

"Every lighthouse has its odor, carefully indicated on the marine maps. I have rose lighthouses, lemon lighthouses, musk lighthouses. At the top of each lighthouse, a powerful atomizer sprays these odors toward the sea. Nothing simpler, then, to orient yourself. In a fog, the captain opens his nostrils, and confirms, for example, that an aroma of cloves is arriving from the north-north-west, and an aroma of mignonette from the southeast. By consulting his map, he can determine his exact position. Eh?"

"Wonderful! And there's something you didn't think of. I'll give you my idea for nothing: when you have a lighthouse situated on the rocks, construct it of some strong cheese like Livarot, you could smell that for miles; and if some tempest, as often happens, prevents the delivery of provisions, well, the keepers won't starve: they can eat their lighthouse."

The funny little man shot me a look of contempt, and changed the subject.

RUSSIAN CRIME

At the drop of a hat.
DOSTOEVSKY

.   .   .   .

t was the very intensity of the old woman's ugliness, I believe, that drew me to her.

When, passing through some sinister and transversal alley, I noticed her at the window, that detestable hag, with her wan purplish face, her beady eyes shining with every filthy lust, and her frizzy brown wig, so obviously fake, my brain was flooded with a blast of that vile lubricity that haunts the daydreams of certain very young men and some disgusting old ones.

Up close, she was repugnant beyond description.

The rosacea on her old sagging cheeks was aggravated by coarse powder acquired from some eleventh-class herbalist, probably an abortionist.

Successive repairs to her enormous dentures had left teeth of mottled blue beside others that looked like old ivory.

And if, at that moment, I had not been so calm in my mind, I would have certainly thought myself the plaything of some harrowing nightmare.

※

It was not poverty that drove her to practice her foul profession, for everything, in her room, exuded almost comfortable affluence.

Fine white sheets garnished the bed, a bed for wealthy city folk. A Norman wardrobe of massive oak sat in one corner of the room, with that rich appearance, that appearance — which reason cannot explain — of being filled, which makes "people like me" infallibly distinguish filled wardrobes from empty ones, even when closed.

In a crapuliform voice that she tried to make lilting, the old woman chatted with me. She complimented my hat.

"What a beautiful hat!"

As a matter of fact, my hat, an old present that General Sakapharine gave to me in Plevna, was more beautiful than human language could express.

I tasted the joy of contradicting the old woman:

"My hat! It is ignoble; I paid thirty-five sous for it, this morning, to a man who collects cigar butts on the place Maubert."

"Nasty joker!"

As the conversation continued in this vein, the idea occurred to me, a vague urge at first, to kill this woman at the drop of a hat.

And I muttered, under my breath, those words: at the drop of a hat.

At that point, the decision to murder the old woman took hold of me, irremissibly. I dropped my hat.

My knife was one of those known as Nontron knives, which are manufactured in Châtellerault.

The blade of the knife is straight and sharp. The well-rounded handle narrows at the base to fit the hand, and a wide removable ferrule prevents the blade from snapping shut.

At one moment, the old woman turned her back. I drove the knife, very hard and very straight, into a place that I know.

As she crumpled to her knees in a helpless position, I kept the knife in the wound, and the wide ferrule stopped the blood from flowing.

When she had cried her last hoarse "ooh," when the internal hemorrhaging had finally stifled her, I took from a drawer in the wardrobe some gold coins and a few valuables, and, closing the door behind me, walked away...

The whole scene had not lasted ten minutes, with no noise, no blood spilled.

Certainly, for a job well done, as the poet Sarcey says, she was a job well done.[1]

※

I headed for the house of my mistress, a young woman named Nini, whom all my friends had nicknamed Nini Novgorod, once I had become her lover.

A pair of policemen were walking slowly toward me.

I don't know why, but their calm expressions sent an icy shiver over the surface of my skin. They seemed too calm.

So, shamelessly, I gazed boldly into their eyes, and both, as if moved by mechanical impulse, raised, as they passed, their hands to the brims of their kepis.

Other police officers that I met further on, and stared at in the same way, also saluted me, responding to my secret preoccupation.

"You seem so unlike a murderer," they seemed to say, "dear sir, that we will not hesitate to salute you respectfully."

※

Nini Novgorod was not at home. Mechanically, I glanced at the mirror in the salon, and was then shaken by the most joyous burst of laughter, perhaps, of my whole life.

I discovered the explanation for my sudden respect from the guardians of the peace.

The ferrule on my knife had not hermetically sealed the old woman's wound.

Through the gap in the handle, which permitted the blade to close, had spurted a thin stream of blood.

The stream had spread into the shape of a rosette, on the buttonhole

---

1. "Job" is feminine in Russian.

of my frock coat.

All those imbeciles had mistaken me for an officer of the Legion of Honor.

ALPHONSKI ALLAISOFF.

NEWS ITEMS
SUMMER SQUIBS

A letter received last week from Chalon-sur-Saône continues to cut me to the quick.

My surly correspondent asks me *quosque tandem*, will I bore him with my tedious cock-and-bull stories. He denies me any ingenuity in my observations. Imagination, in his opinion, forever eludes my grasp.

He adds coldly that my style is brackish and cabaretesque.

All these reproaches would be nothing without a venomous postscript — a postal Parthian shot — in which he brutally adds:

"To fool the reader is an easy art. I will bet, dear sir, that you are too *goddam* (sic) incompetent to turn out a simple news item."

To this last reproach, I must admit, my heart skipped a beat (more than one). I dipped my excellent Toledo pen into the inkwell, and composed, in less time than it takes to write it, a small batch of news items which, in my humble opinion, are not just something you would put in a vase.

Ever since Laffitte became a minister for having picked up a pin in the courtyard of a bank, I pick up everything, even challenges.

Here is my modest attempt:

PROBABLE WEATHER TOMORROW

Dry with a chance of rain. Relatively elevated temperatures, barring a thermometric declivity.

❈

THE ACCIDENT AT RUE QUINCAMPOIX

A young carpenter named Edmond Q..., 48 years old, was engaged in replacing the slates on the roof of a building at 328 rue Mazagran, when, after a dizzy spell, he was precipitated into the void.

The accident had attracted a considerable crowd, and there was a general cry of horror from the onlookers.

The unfortunate man was expected to strike the pavement, when, as he passed a second floor window, what was the surprise of the crowd to see the worker, solicited by a wink from a woman of easy virtue, and who abound in this neighborhood, stop his fall and climb through the window into the prostitute's room.

The doctors will make no announcement about his condition until a week has passed.

※

THE NEW CARS ON THE WESTERN RAILWAY

A good idea from the Western Railway. They have just put into circulation new cars for snuff takers. A copper plaque, engraved with the words "Snuff Takers," indicates the purpose of these cars.

It will be forbidden from now on to take snuff in compartments other than those reserved ad hoc.

Beginning on July 1, all first-class cars will be equipped with "ice bottles," which are nothing but hot water bottles in which the hot water is replaced by ice.

It is to be hoped that similar measures will apply to second-class cars, and even third-class.

Let us close with some good news.

The Western Railway is finally responding to incessant complaints from its engineers.

Next winter, on all the major lines, the locomotives will be heated.

※

BICYCLES AGAIN

The Police Commissioner, instead of pursuing bookmakers and innocent little flower girls, would do much better to think of controlling *bicycles, which, in this warm weather, constitute a real public danger.*

Again, yesterday morning, a bicycle escaped from its hangar and traveled down the rue Vivienne at top speed, knocking into everything and sowing terror in its passage.

It had reached the corner of the boulevard Montparnasse and the rue Lepic, when a brave patrolman brought it down with a bullet in the left pedal.

The autopsy determined that it was afflicted with rabies.

A handcart that it had bitten was immediately taken to the Pasteur Institute.

WHERE WILL FRAUD HIDE NEXT!

The authorities have just arrested and taken to the station a coalman, named Gandillot, who had found an excellent gimmick for making money at the expense of the purse and health of his clientele.

This honest individual delivered to his customers, instead of the water they had ordered, a local wine from his hometown that he bought at a discount.

The fraud was soon discovered, thanks to the indisposition of an old woman of Polish origin, the widow Mazur K..., rentier, who sent the dubious liquid to a municipal laboratory.

The stalwart worker from Auvergne will have to explain his ingenious scheme to the judge.

ACCIDENTAL LOWERING OF THE SEINE

A strange and, fortunately, rather rare accident has just caused some consternation among all those who live along the Seine.

An enormous barge, loaded with blotting paper, collided with one of the piers of the Pont Royal. It sprang a leak, and sank immediately.

The blotting paper contained in the barge soon absorbed all the surrounding water, causing a decrease of 1.20 meters in the river's low-

water mark.

The fire brigade stationed on la rue Blanche, summoned without delay, arrived and set to work to return everything to its former condition.

After six hours of relentless work, the Seine regained its normal level.

Unfortunately, the brave firemen, in their zeal, also caused a great deal of damage.

Let us mention in particuar the Deligny bathhouse, which was literally inundated.

A bit less zeal, please!

Well, my dear citizen of Châlon, am I too *goddam* (sic) incompetent to write a news item, yes or no?

DRUM CLASS

"**G**ood Lord!" I exclaimed. "It will not be said that I passed so close to Lemballeur without stopping to say hello!"

Two hours after this cordial monologue, a rented car, costly but unmerciful to the buttocks of this poor world, deposited me before the fort of C...

From a sentiment of discretion that all true patriots will appreciate, I will not give the location of the fort of C..., nor its strategic value, its resources, its objectives, its weaknesses — despite the fact that these revelations would probably be met with blizzards of thalers from the other side of the Rhine; I don't care: I would rather take the bus with my three French sous than ride in luxury with Teutonic gold. (Are you happy, Déroulède?)

I will content myself, and it will suffice, with saying that the fort in question is occupied by a company of infantry and a few vague soldiers from the supply train.

The company is commanded by Captain Lemballeur, an old friend of mine, who cannot proffer four words without interjecting "Hellfire and damnation!" two or three times. Moreover, the best son in the world, and a father to his men.

Delighted to see me, Captain Lemballeur, hellfire and damnation!, introduced me to his lieutenant, a merry and punhappy fellow, and to his second lieutenant, a young officer of great promise.

These gentlemen were charming. We at once became the best of friends.

Lemballeur, while awaiting lunch, insisted that I visit the fort's garden, a garden where they grew carrots, hellfire and damnation!, as big as that, and amazing cabbages, old man!

After that, I was asked to contemplate the fort's rabbits, strapping rabbits indeed, and the fort's chickens, poultry second to none.

They had reserved, for the finale, the spectacle of the fort's pig, a pig named Auguste, who was the object of the whole company's idolatry.

To speak frankly, the pig looked to me like every other pig in the world, but before the enthusiasm of those fine men, I admitted, with exquisite grace, that Auguste was a very remarkable pig, a pig perhaps one of a kind, even one of all kinds.

Although fully fattened long ago, Auguste escaped execution: nobody in the company would have consented to kill him. The captain, besides, hellfire and damnation!, had never ordered such a murder.

We might still be admiring Auguste to this day, if a man had not come to inform us that the officers were summoned to the table.

Excellent menu. Healthy and abundant food. And then, fresh air, the mountains... What an appetite, my good sirs!

After lunch, Lemballeur slipped his arm in mine.

"Let's go see the fort's grounds, hellfire and damnation!"

And the excellent captain said "the fort's grounds" in the same tone he had said "the fort's rabbits." In his mind, the grounds had been created and set upon this earth specifically for the beautification of his fort.

They were, in fact, something to be proud of.

I have seen many grounds in my life, but have never encountered any to compare with the grounds of Lemballeur's fort.

Rocks, pine forests, streams, waterfalls, the whole gamut.

You almost thought you were in one of those mechanical and pendulum-bearing pictures they make in Tyrol. All that was missing was a little train in the back.

Ah! It was hard to tear ourselves away from such a picturesque scene, but time is time and business is business.

As we returned to the fort, the loud sound of drumming burst out suddenly not far from us.

"Huh!" Lemballeur said proudly. "Do you hear that drumming?"

The fort's two drummers, Larigouille, full-size drummer, and Peloteux, student drummer, were, according to the captain, the best drummers in the world.

"Do you hear them?" repeated Lemballeur. "They drum! They drum! Hellfire and damnation! You'd think they were a whole regiment."

But the captain's bewilderment passed all limits, when he saw that it was Larigouille alone who was making all the racket.

Where was Peloteux? Mystery! Certainly not far away, for his drum lay there, at Larigouille's feet.

And Larigouille kept drumming, multiplying the strokes of his sticks, with the obvious intention of giving the illusion of many simultaneous drummers.

Where the devil was Peloteux, all this time?

"Ah, there he is!" I cried. "Well, he doesn't look too bored!"

Pelotuex, in fact, was not at all bored.

Very relaxed, in his shirtsleeves, Peloteux was flirting with a young shepherdess whose flock grazed not far from there, unaware of their mistress's turpitudes.

When I say that Peloteux was "flirting," I beg the reader to see in this term merely a euphemism due to my extreme discretion, for if the Prince of Wales ever "flirted" that way with Lady Namitt in the salon (do not print "saloon") of Windsor, I can imagine the face of the Empress of India. I don't have to explain further, do I?

A pretty girl, that herdswoman. Her features, tanned by the sun, contrasted markedly with her torso, which appeared plump, copious, and thoroughly white.

And Larigouille kept drumming!

Here below, all things must end, Peloteux's "flirting" along with everything else.

The lovers arose from their couch of pink heather, and made a few corrections to their attire. The shepherdess's blouse, notably, required a less disheveled arrangement.

Peloteux put on his jacket, and, after a final kiss for the young woman, rejoined Larigouille, who had still not stopped his racket.

Already charmed by this idyllic vision, we witnessed a second act even more charming than the first.

In a fraction of a second, Peloteux had regained possession of his drum, and Larigouille had rid himself of his.

Peloteux attacked a "quick march" capable of leading ten thousand men to victory.

Larigouille was already "flirting" with the herdswoman.

(For more about this "flirting," please refer to the observation made above.)

"Hellfire and damnation! She's a lively one!" murmured Lemballeur, quite inflamed.

In this circumstance, the student drummer Peloteux showed himself charmingly witty and appropriate.

The "quick march" lasted the proper time that it should last; it was replaced by the "charge," a heroic and decisive charge. Then a great drumroll, confused and chaotic. One could picture a host of defeated angels, tumbling into an abyss of ecstasy!

Then another drumroll, but a soft and melancholy drumroll, that one, the drumroll of the dousing of the flames.

Then Chloë took up her crook, gave a last glance at her two Daphnises in red pants, like a good girl, and pushed her lambkins on, toward elsewhere.

Very pleased with their completed duties, the drummers lined up with comic gravity, counted off, did an about-face, and returned to the fort to the sound of the retreat.

Lemballeur was beside himself. If I had not happened to be there, he would have certainly run after the young woman of the mountains, but his dignity!...

"Very smart, hellfire and damnation! Those drummers!" he concluded. "Very smart to drum for both of them when the other has nasty work to do."

I corrected that last expression, and jumped into the officers' car after a cordial handshake with those gentlemen.

.   .   .   .

Before leaving the area, I wanted to say goodbye to my old friend Lemballeur, and so I returned to the fort.

"And the drummers?" I asked.

"If you'd like to see them, we don't have far to go. Come with me."

At the end of a corridor was a room, stinking of iodoform. It was the infirmary.

The drummers were drinking couch grass.

TOM

We were discussing dogs.

"Me," said the first, "I saw a dog that did this."

"Me," replied the second, "my grandfather had a dog that did that."

"Me," added the third (a certain Bonnet), "I knew a guy in Lille whose dog did this and that."

Up to that point, the laurels rested securely with two dogs, both remarkable.

The first, it appeared, went out every morning to fetch, from the nearest newsstand, its owner's favorite papers, *L'Intransigeant* and *La Presse*. (This was at the height of the Boulanger period.)

The very day that the brave general put the Franco-Belgian border between himself and a well-known magistrate, the good little doggie, thoroughly disgusted with this pusillanimity, brought his master some Anti-Boulanger gazette, I forget which.

A few lashes of the riding crop from the owner, who remained faithful to his idol.

The next day, our poodle, more and more resolute in his horror for the tinhorn Caesar, firmly refused to bring back the dictatorial organs.

Tired of fighting, the gentleman surrendered, and had to start reading the governmental, or at least independent, press.

For the second dog, we give the floor to its master.

"The day that my wife lost her poor mother (God save the soul of that appalling old shrew!), everything in the house was topsy-turvy. My wife was weeping, and I could scarcely believe my luck. In short, we forgot to set out a dish for poor Black. (We called him Black because he was all white.) What do you think he did?"

"He howled miserably?"

"Oh! Far from it! Black went into the garden, and came back carrying, in his mouth, a sprig of myosotis."

(Myosotis has always been considered a plant as memoriferous as the devil. Thus, the Germans call it *forget me not* — *don't forget me* would be more grammatical — the French call it *vergiss mein nicht,* and the English *ne m'oubliez pas.*)

Plaudits were shared between the dog with the myosotis and the Anti-Boulanger dog, when Miss Sarbah Kahn, a young Englishwoman, Jewish, redheaded, with strangely piercing black eyes, none too pretty, but so very delightful, asked:

"And you, the keeper of belfry bats, you don't say a word. Have you ever known an amazing dog?"

The keeper of belfry bats, thus questioned, answered in a weary voice:

"Amazing dogs? I've known them as no one else has. One in particular."

Perceiving that our curiosity was overexcited to its highest point, the keeper of belfry bats stopped, astute raconteur that he was.

"So, your dog..." pleaded Sarbah Kahn.

"My dog? Ah yes, my amazing dog, Well, his name was Tom."

"And... that's all?"

"I can say no more before a lady."

"But I'm not a lady," riposted Sarbah, "I'm a young woman."

"Well, that's different."

And this is how the keeper of belfry bats told us the story of Tom:

I forget what year it was. Besides, the date is unimportant: if my story had happened in the days of the Capetians, it would lose none of its savor.

I fulfilled, in that epoch, the delicate duties of a chemistry assistant in the Abnormal School. It was in this capacity that I was sent by a rich capitalist to the little town of Toutaleuil, to establish a factory for indigenous rubber.

Because, as you know, or rather as you seem not to know, France could easily stop being dependent on South America for its rubber and gutta-percha.

Reread my doctoral thesis and you will see that mignonette pistils secrete, for about a week in the year, a substance similar to rubber, with the added benefit of being spongy and perfectly permeable.

It must have been six thirty when I arrived at the Toutaleuil station, and seven o'clock when the bus deposited me before the Three Hemispheres Hotel.

Dinner was served.

So as not to offend anyone's beliefs, I did as they.

I will always remember that the tapioca had a slightly moldy flavor, rather unpleasant for those of us who do not enjoy mold.

After dinner, a tour of the not particularly lively cafes in Toutaleuil.

The customers were playing piquet... "And the last nine!"

Paul Marrot was right when he said:

The rhythm of the engine, as it clacks across the ties,
May cause a certain gentle stirring, in between the thighs.

On my return to the hotel, at the stroke of ten, I felt the pangs of solitude. *Vae soli!* said the Preacher, who knew all about it.

A quick conversation with the manager of the Three Hemispheres told me that the valiant little town of Toutaleuil harbored — lower your eyes, Miss Sarbah — two nocturnal refuges for solitary men, and in those refuges... But you understand. The slightest insistence on the subject would be unpardonably tactless, even boorish.

"Is it far?" I asked.

"Five minutes... Besides, Tom will lead you."

And from the window, the manager whistled, and called:

"Tom! Tom! Tom!"

Tom did not take long to appear.

He arrived, jumping, joyful, bearing no grudge for his interrupted sleep.

"Take the gentleman to number 7."

We set out together, Tom leading me gravely, as if proud of his mission.

And, during the trip, I thought to myself:

"A strange destiny, all the same, that of this Newfoundland leading me to debauchery." (Tom was a purebred Newfoundland.)

Atavism, perhaps! Who knows if Tom's mother, roaming her native shore, had ever cast a glance at some frisky sailor hoping to butter his bread — for there is such a thing as anchovy butter — by fishing for hookers among the many in the area.

Who knows?...

I was at that point in my reflections, when I saw, several meters ahead of me, two red lanterns cutting through the night.

The first was a bright scarlet, rich, triumphant, a red that seemed like a trumpet call.

The other lantern was a faded vermilion, a vermilion fallen into pissy oranges, a miserable and destitute red.

On the glass of these lanterns were enormous numbers, true presbyopic digits.

The opulent scarlet bore the number 7. The poverty-stricken vermilion indicated 14.

Tom stopped before the 7.

At his joyous barking, the door opened, opened wide with friendly welcome and courteous hospitality.

The woman who received me carefully relocked the door, and cried up the stairwell:

"Come down, ladies! It's Tom!"

I don't know who they fussed over more, Tom or me.

Madame ordered that Tom be brought the skeleton of a freshly devoured chicken, while I selected a little brunette whom I thought was as funny as could be, and who was as stupid as her feet.

After this regrettable discovery, I rejoined my friend Tom, who was busily lapping up beer from a soup bowl.

All of the ladies were after him, pampering him, petting him, calling him their good doggie, their pretty Tomtom, their dear little bow-wow. The madam was no less attentive.

"You seem very fond of this dog?"

"For good reason, monsieur. Tom brings us plenty of clients, and never any deadbeats!"

"But..."

"No, monsieur, never any deadbeats! If any show up among the tourists, he sniffs them out and takes them to number 14."

IN ANOTHER MAN'S SKIN

We were at dessert or maybe even coffee and maybe even still further, when one of our fellow guests, the occultist Jean Fourié, whom we never fail to call, as is only right, Sâr Jean Fourié, raised the question of the Rosy + Cross.

Everything that could pass for a table in the apartment began, without delay, to waltz around like dead leaves, to the great disadvantage of the china, which, as a result, was soon strewn over the floor in enough quantity to generate entire volumes of Sully-Prudhomme.

(Me, I didn't care, so empty was my glass.)

Magic, cabala, Satanism, Theosophy, esotericism, Péladan, Paul Adam, Up and Adam, hereafter, elsewhere, not here, down there, all enameled the most contentious of conversations.

The spiritualists' eyes shone as if with an inner fire, and the materialists coldly shrugged their shoulders.

As for those who were indifferent, their attitude consisted of swigging glasses of Irish whiskey, as if it were raining the stuff.

And as far as I was concerned, if that detail holds any interest, I found myself simultaneously spiritualist, materialist, and indifferent. (There are days when one is in form.)

Wasn't force really just a property of matter?

And I began to have my doubts about it all, crazed with anguish. Could there be, who knows, insubstantial spirits, strolling through our surroundings? What then?

A fresh glass of whiskey soothed me somewhat, while the Sâr Jean Fourié went on to chat about Buddhism, avatars, and other things.

One could, he affirmed, remove the self from the body like a simple pocket handkerchief, and transport it into the perishable envelope of another human, whose soul you would then inherit, during the operation.

At that, a materialist in the group lost his patience and cried:

"You bunch of... simpletons!" (It was even another word that he used.) "You bunch of... simpletons! Trucking souls around! That only proves your theories are right, because your heads are filled with the spirits of idiots. Tell me right now, while you're at it, that you could make the tolling of the great bell at Notre-Dame emigrate into this dinner bell! You bunch of... simpletons!"

(I must repeat that it was another word that he used.)

※

Among those who made themselves conspicuous by their silence, I will especially note our fine American friend, Harry Covayre.

Harry Covayre was directing, for the moment, all of his energies into confecting whiskey toddies, mixtures that contained relatively little sugar, and, so to speak, almost no water.

"And you, Harry," one of us asked, "do you believe in avatars?"

"If anyone here wants me to drop dead, just mention the subject. It reminds me of the most terrifying period of my life..."

"!!!???...!!!" we all cried simultaneously.

"Oh, for God's sake," continued Harry, obviously deeply upset, "never speak to me of the transmigration of the self."

"!!!...!!!" we insisted.

"Such as you see me now, I have walked an entire day in Paris, in another man's skin, a man I didn't know from Adam, or Eve (Ning). Do you think that was agreeable?"

"Tell us about it, Harry."

And Harry was quite willing to tell us about it.

※

It was about a year ago.

Like today, we had spent the whole night with a friend in the Latin Quarter, discussing all things supernatural, or supposedly so.

We had turned tables, we had invoked spirits, who were very nice, my word, and very obliging. Apparently they're none too busy in the other world, for, at our first summons, all those gentlemen, Homer, Alcibiades, Jesus Christ, Saint Thomas, Louis-Phillipe, the late Bloomer, put themselves at our disposition, as graciously as we could wish.

Having recently arrived in Paris, I was intensely upset by this kind of exercise, and, at dawn, slipped quietly away.

To say that I had not had a few drinks, during the seance, would be a baldfaced lie. In short, I felt all funny, as soon as the fresh air of the street hit my face.

I went down the rue Saint-Jacques and found myself before the morgue.

Mechanically, I went in.

Horror of horrors, the first corpse that I saw on the cold slab was my little girlfriend of the time, a fine woman who cheated on me with the entire Left Bank. (It was that, I think, that endeared her to me.)

Epouvantabile visu!

White-faced, I rushed into the office.

"Monsieur," I said, "I know that young woman..."

"Your declaration is useless, monsieur, we found papers on her that establish her identity. She was drowned with her lover, as it says in a letter..."

"But me, I'm her lover!"

"No, monsieur, it was the young man lying on the next slab."

Curiosity won over sorrow, and I went to contemplate the features of my rival.

Now, my rival, do you know who it was?

No, you don't know!

It was me, ME!

I felt as if my head were cracking open.

The stiff that I had before my eyes, was actually ME, and his clothes were actually MINE.

"All right," I said to myself, "calm down."

And I said to the clerk in the calmest tone I could muster:

"That young man looks so much like me! Don't you think?"

The clerk burst out laughing:

"He looks like you about as much as I look like the pope."

I dashed to the office mirror.

The reflected image was of a tall pale young man with black sideburns. (You can see how much that resembles me.)

I took a look at the clothes I was wearing. I was dressed in a gray checked suit, which I never remembered wearing.

The papers tucked into the wallet were those of a young Spaniard, totally unknown to me.

I, or rather my body, was dead, and my soul was now in this imbecile.

And I who knew not a word of Spanish!

Ah, what fun!

Can you imagine my situation?

I was exhausted.

But where could I go to bed, where?

At his place? At mine?

At my place, I'd be turned away.

At his place... what would his wife say, or his children, when they saw that I didn't speak Spanish.

I had his address, his street, his number. But what floor?

Impossible to ask the concierge, who would think I'd suddenly gone mad.

And then what to say to his wife? What to say to her!

Oh my God!

I've had many troubles in the course of my existence, but never as many as that day.

I went to the places I used to frequent.

Naturally, nobody recognized me.

On the other hand, several strangers greeted me, shook my hand, talked about a lot of mysterious things which I answered who knows how.

I went to have a drink at the Café de la Paix, where a waiter immediately brought me the *Epoca*.

Then two men passing in a car spotted me; they stopped, and one of them handed me a thousand francs, which he must have owed the other man, while jabbering in some bizarre jargon.

My God, my God, what an existence opened up before me!

I quickly made up my mind:

"I will kill myself tomorrow."

But realizing how stupid it would be to kill myself with fifty louis in my pocket (plus a dozen more in that preliminary wallet), I threw myself into the most Byzantine orgies.

My God, what memories!

. . . .

❋

As if those memories were strangling him, Harry Covayre downed in one gulp a copious whiskey toddy, in which there was no sugar whatsoever, and even less water.

"And how long was it," one of us asked, "before your soul returned to its own envelope?"

Harry answered coldly:

"Not until the next morning, when I sobered up."

CONSOLATRIX

How stupid we are when we're young, all the same!

Of course, as we grow older... But I must stop, as this qualification has nothing to do with the story that follows.

A long time ago, a very long time ago — how far away it is, all that! — my heart was broken.

Don't laugh, you heartless rabble, truly broken, with real distress, with raving anger. Not to mention that I was as hurt as a turkey.

A little girlfriend of mine, whose name was Hélène (I think her name was Hélène), left me to yoke herself to the destiny of a sinister and shadowy Romanian, who studied medicine — although I always wondered when he found the time.

I cannot recall ever being so unhappy in any other period of my sorry existence.

During the day, my pain was still bearable. I came, I went, I drank a bit too much: in short, I managed to dull myself, more or less.

But at night!

Oh, the agonizing returns to the empty room! The photographs that I hypnotized myself with until they seemed to move! The letters I read for the eleven hundred thousandth time! O sorrowfulness! O funereality!

My evenings were as strictly ruled out as music paper.

As soon as I returned, as soon as my lamp was lit, I collapsed, like a calf, onto my bed, and I wept, I wept, trying to muffle, in the pillows, my convulsive sobs.

After a few minutes, somewhat calmed, I dried my eyes, and gave myself over to the long contemplation of HER portraits, of which I had an abundant supply.

Without being pretty in the true sense of the word, Hélène

Was, in every way, an object of desire,

as the poet Paul Harel said.

I loved her eyes, not very large but so droll, with occasionally a spark of tenderness, her mocking little nose, her savory ripe mouth, the like of which, since then, I have never found again.

So, I told myself that all those treasures were lost to me: despair wrung my heart, my poor heart, and... off again on a second round of convulsive sobs!

※

One evening, I had reached that point in my routine, when I heard a little *ratatap* at my door.

(To express someone knocking at the door, English writers do not use our onomatopoeia *toc-toc*, they say *ratatap*, and I don't find it so ridiculous.)

A great emotional upheaval shook my being to the marrow.

What if it were her!

"Who is it?"

"Me, monsieur," said the soft thin voice of a child.

"Who are you?"

"The little girl of the lady who lives next to you."

I opened the door.

The blonde head of an adorably pretty little girl, seven or eight years old, appeared in the gap.

"Are you sick, monsieur?"

"Me? Not at all. Why?"

"Because I heard you crying for an hour."

"No, I'm not sick. I was crying because I was in pain."

"Ah!"

"But come in, you'll catch cold in the hallway. Did your mama send you?"

"Oh no, mama isn't here. She won't be back tonight."

What a funny little girl, intelligent, sensitive, and no bigger than a mouse!

She made me tell my story, and was very interested.

"Oh," she said, "I've seen your little lady, with a little otter skin coat, right? And a gray hat that's got a bird with claws. I met her several times on the stairs."

"Yes, that's her."

"But she doesn't seem bad."

"I didn't say she was bad, but she left me anyway."

"Ah! Bah, she'll come back, you wait and see!'

Then the poor kid, in turn, told me her story, which was none too cheery.

Her mother, a waitress in the brasserie of d'Harcourt, had sent her to be raised in the country, but since her monthly board arrived at increasingly unpredictable intervals, the farmer had returned the child, who lived thereafter in the hotel room, next to mine.

That night, the mother, who seemed to me insufficiently concerned, was not due back.

It was getting late. I urged my little friend to go to bed.

"Oh! I'm not very sleepy."

"That doesn't matter, go to bed; even more so, since if anyone saw you over here at this time of night..."

"All right, good night!"

And then, after a brief pause:

"All the same, it's too bad I'm not bigger!"

"Why?"

"Because... then I could really console you!"

Poor kid! She was so sweet when she said that. Not depraved for a sou, but of such an affectionate nature!

She left, leaving me brooding, and how.

✻

The next day, unable to stay any longer in that room still perfumed by my absent love — oh, the slut! — I moved out.

Musset once said that neither absence nor time matter when one is in love.

Villemer and Delormel affirmed that "You don't die of love" (*bis*)

Villemer and Delormel were right.

Time soon spread upon my ulcerated heart the arnica of oblivion.

One nail drives out another; one woman, too.

✻

Last week, I found myself in Le Havre.

A little yacht returned to port, coming in to dock. The little yacht was called the *Salt Herring*, and I immediately recognized the owner, that imbecile Puyjûteux.

He introduced me to his mistress, a smart and exquisite little blonde, no bigger than two dabs of butter, but so funny!

And while Puyjûteux gave, in his most "old salt" tone, a few orders to his crew, the little blonde asked me tranquilly:

"Well, are you consoled now?"

"Consoled about what?"

She reminded me of the facts.

"What? You were that little girl?"

And I pretended to be still in pain, so that she might console me, now that she was grown up, that little girl.

FOOLISHNESS

The man was staring at me so intently that I started to lose my temper. I came close to giving him a good couple of slaps in the physiognomy, not to mention a kick in the gums.

"Are you done looking at me, you imbecile?" I cried, overcome with rage.

But he arose, walked over to me, and took my hands with every mark of affection.

"Is it really you talking to me like that?" he said.

I didn't recognize him at all.

His name was: Edmond Tirouard.

"What?" I exclaimed. "It's you, my poor Tirouard! I couldn't place you. But excuse me, if I may, back then weren't you blond with blue eyes?"

"That's right, I had my hair and eyes dyed. Don't I look better in brown?"

Poor old Tirouard, I was so happy to see him again! It had been so long!

And we plucked our memories from the past.

And So-and-So? And Whatsisname? And Whosis? Alas! So many gone!

Tirouard and I, we were in the same class at school. I don't remember exactly which of us was lazier, but what laughs we had!

He pillaged the house of his father, who ran a hardware store, and every morning brought us a thousand little agreeable and useful objects: knives, screws, padlocks, magnets (I adored magnets).

And I, in my capacity as a pharmacist's son, I gorged my friends with sacks of rubbish: cough drops, dates. Sometimes I brought glass syringes (what joy!) and athletic supporters, which we made into slingshots.

One day — my God, how I laughed that day! — I arrived provided with a box of cookies, each containing, if memory serves, seventy-five centigrams of a powerful laxative.

The whole class swallowed those treacherous treats in one mouthful, but an hour later you should have seen their white little faces. My God, how I laughed!

Ah! That day, the grade point averages didn't rise much in our class.

How long ago it was, all that!

And Tirouard and I, we looked back on those vanished times.

"Do you remember my experiment with the parachute?"

Did I remember his parachute!

One Thursday, in the afternoon, Tirouard invited us to an experiment that had sprung from his ingenuity.

He had attached a basket to the handle of an old red umbrella, introduced a cat into the basket, and released it to the pleasure of the winds.

The pleasure of the winds floated the device through the air for several hours. The whole town was in an uproar.

Tirouard's aunt, who adored her cat, and had never envisioned such a fate for it, emitted wails that would have melted precious stones.

At last, the device got caught on the steeple cock, and it took no less then a corporal of the fire brigade to rescue the aerial kitty.

"And now," I asked Tirouard, "what do you do?"

"I do nothing, my friend: I'm rich."

And Tirouard was eager to recount his existence, an existence that made old Homer's Odyssey seem like an insipid fireside anecdote.

A few striking episodes from Tirouard's story will give my clientele some idea of my friend's originality.

Certain unsuccessful enterprises (among others the "Continental Fish Market," rejected by the major fishmongers of Paris), resolved my friend to expatriate.

His trinket business hardly fared better.

Still young, and frivolous and impulsive by nature, he did not always pay attention to whether the merchandise he exported met the needs of the receiving country.

He managed to send, for example, Japanese fans to Spitzberg, and bedwarmers to the Congo.

Disgusted with commerce, he left for Canada in the hope of entering merchant banking. Hard times lay ahead, and he was compelled, to support himself, to embrace the profession of deep-sea diving.

Divers were cruelly exploited at that time. Tirouard gathered them into a union, and organized a general strike of the deep-sea divers of the Saint Lawrence.

A rather curious fact in the history of strikes: those intrepid workers demanded neither an augmentation of salary nor a diminution of labor.

All that they asked was the absolute right not to work in the rain.

Let us add that they quickly won their battle.

After that, Tirouard devoted himself to training all sorts of animals. His efforts were crowned with success.

Tirouard trained all the animals in creation, from the elephant to the cheese mite.

But it was especially in the training of canned sardines that he surpassed all that had been done before.

Nothing was more interesting than to see those intelligent little creatures maneuver, frisk about, and perform a thousand tricks in their aquarium.

The show ended with the soldiers' chorus from Faust, sung by the sardines, after which they tucked themselves into their cans, where they remained until the next day's performance.

Today, Tirouard, rich and an officer in the Academy, enjoys a rest that he has richly earned.

Yesterday, I visited his marvelous mansion on the Impasse de Guelma, where I particularly admired the hanging gardens he had ordered from Babylon, at great expense.

POST OFFICE

I got off the train at Baisemoy-en-Cort, where the dogcart of my old friend Lenfileur awaited me.

On the train, I had remembered an unpardonable oversight (truly unpardonable), and my first order of business, when I disembarked, was to have myself taken to the post office, so that I could send a telegram to Paris.

The Baisemoy-en-Cort post office is remarkable for an absence of comfort that verges on destitution.

In an ink that was faded and mildewed, but muddy, I dipped an old antique pen, and scrawled, with great difficulty, the characters whose ensemble constituted my telegram.

A woman, rather ugly, received it without graciousness, counted the words, and indicated a sum that I deposited forthwith on the counter.

I was about to retire with the satisfaction of a duty accomplished, when I saw in the office, her back to me, a young woman occupied in feverishly tapping out Morse code.[1]

Young? Probably. Redhead? Absolutely. Pretty? Why not!

Her black dress, very simple, clung to a pretty figure that was both plump and clearly understood.

Her copious hair, gathered into a twist on the top of her head, revealed the nape of her neck, a divine neck, light amber, where there came to die, way down at the base, a delicate little fleece, curly — one might even say insubstantial.

---

1. To avoid all confusion, the "Morse" in question is a device for telegraphic transmission named after its inventor, and does not refer to the French, or archaic English, term for "walrus." The presence of the latter, frequent in glacial seas, is, moreover, rare in French post offices.

(If the soul has hair, it must be like the hair on that neck.)

And an urge overwhelmed me, sudden, irrational, mad, to plant a kiss on the telegraphist's little pale golden curls.

In the hope that the young person would eventually turn around, I stood there, at the window, asking the clerk administrative questions that she answered without courtesy.

But the neck kept transmitting.

At the post office door, my friend Lenfileur was growing impatient. (His little mare is a spirited one.)

I went away.

※

It would be to misjudge me strangely, not to guess that the next morning, bright and early, I presented myself at the post office.

She was there, the beautiful redhead, and alone.

This time she was quite obliged to show me her face. I had no complaints, for it was worthy of the neck.

And black eyes, besides, immense ones.

(Oh, the black eyes of redheads!)

I bought stamps, I sent telegrams, I inquired about delivery times: in short, for a good quarter of an hour, I played perfectly the role of a passionate idiot.

She answered me calmly, composedly, with all the air of a sweet and reasonable young woman.

And I went back every day, and even twice a day, for I had finally figured out her working hours, and I scrupulously avoided missing that rendezvous, to which I alone, alas, was invited.

To make my visits seem plausible, I wrote letters to my friends, to mere acquaintances.

In particular, I sent several telegrams to people who probably thought I had gone insane.

Never in my life have I indulged in such an orgy of correspondence.

And every day, I said to myself, "Now is the time; this time I'll speak to her."

But every day, her serious expression intimidated me, and, instead of telling her, "Mademoiselle, I love you!" I confined myself to stammering, "One three sou stamp, please, mademoiselle."

✻

The situation was becoming intolerable.

Since my stay was drawing to a close, I resolved to burn my bridges, and risk everything.

I entered the post office, and this is the telegram that I sent to one of my friends:

Coquelin Cadet, 17, boulevard Haussmann, Paris.
I am madly in love with the little redheaded telegraphist in Baisemoy-en-Cort.

I expected to see, at the very least, a blush on her unforgettable white skin.

Well, nothing of the kind!

In her most formal tones, she said these simple words:

"Ninety-five centimes."

Totally demoralized by her imperial calm, I searched myself to settle my telegram.

Not a single coin in my pocket. So, I pulled a thousand franc note from my billfold.[2]

The young woman took it, examined it carefully, felt it...

The inspection must have been favorable, for her face suddenly relaxed into a pretty smile revealing the the most tempting little choppers in creation.

And then, with an expression that was thoroughly Parisian, and even nineteenth arrondissement, she asked me:

"You want change, monsieur?"

---

2. You seem surprised at this?

LONG LIVE LIFE !

HORSE'S ASS

"Your friend Horse's Ass is starting to become a terrible bore," affirmed Tocquard, dropping fully dressed onto his bed.

Nothing could be truer: the terrible Horse's Ass, who, besides, had never been my friend, was starting to become a terrible bore.

As for his real name, he was called Anatole Duveau, and was the son of M. Duveau and Co., wholesale silk traders (former Hondiret building, Duveau and Co.), rue Vivienne, Paris.

For the moment, he exercised the functions of a reserve second lieutenant in the company, where I progressed, for my part, in the capacity of a second class reservist (it was not ability that barred my promotion, but conduct).

From the first day, Duveau earned his nickname of Horse's Ass, and remained a nuisance to us all.

While the officers in active duty treated us like the best fellows in the world, he, Horse's Ass, made a devil of a fuss, exhibiting a zeal that consisted mostly of showering us with the guardhouse, confinement to barracks, and other privileges.

Ah, the swine!

Since we had not come to Lisieux, after all, to sleep in the "box," we resolved, a few reservists and I, to apply the brakes to this frenzied silk merchant, and our procedure richly deserves to be related here.

The colonel, or rather the lieutenant colonel, because the garrison in Lisieux consisted only of the fourth battalion and the store, had authorized all reservists who were married and accompanied by their wives to sleep in town.

Although I was a bachelor at the time (and still am, for that matter), I boldly declared myself a consort, and obtained my authorization.

I need not add that a host of other men in my position acted as I did, and if the Society of Military Beds had the least bit of heart, they would send us a pretty bronze as a sign of gratitude.

Our fine lieutenant colonel had added to his report that reservists sleeping in town were to return to their lodgings as soon as possible after retreat was sounded.

This last clause, of course, we ignored completely.

Once our duties were done, we returned home to devote ourselves to the task of cleanliness, after which we dined. And then we tried vaguely to kill the evening with a concert at the Café Dubois or at the Alcazar (!) on the rue Petite-Couture.

Others of us visited the notorious establishments on the rue du Moulin-à-Tan, but if that's the way our stout lads are preparing to retake Alsace and Lorraine, then "Negative!" as we say in the military.

At first, all went well: the officers rubbed shoulders with us, recognized us, and left us perfectly alone. But then, one evening, our terrible second lieutenant Horse's Ass decided to visit the concert hall.

Then it was a whole other story. Having seen us in the audience, he invited us, without apparent courtesy, to "clear out" immediately if we didn't want to catch four days.

That prospect determined our attitude: we "cleared out."

But we cleared out with rage in our hearts, resolved to exact a brilliant revenge on Horse's Ass.

Which did not take long.

Forty-eight hours after our humiliation, this is what happened at the Café Dubois, at the stroke of nine thirty:

❈

Horse's Ass enters, and casts a circular glance to assure himself there are no "men" in the audience.

As if moved by force of habit, a young man stands, raises his hand awkwardly to the brim of his hat (which is one way to put it), and looks as nervous as a cat.

Horse's Ass gets a gleam in his eye: there's a man at fault!

"What the hell are you doing here, at this hour?"

"But my lieutenant..."

"There's no 'my lieutenant.' Pay and clear out."

"But my lieutenant..."

"Didn't you hear me? Pay and clear out!"

"But my lieutenant, I'm not hurting anyone by drinking a toddy and listening to some good music before going home to bed."

"You know very well that the colonel..."

"The colonel! I don't give a damn about the colonel!"

"You don't give a damn about the colonel!"

"No, I don't give a damn about the colonel, or you either, my dear Horse's Ass!"

That was too much!

Horse's Ass, sputtering with indignation, called over two sergeants who happened to be there, due to a ten o'clock permission.

"Grab that man there and march him back to the barracks!"

"That man there" finished his toddy, paid his bill, and said simply:

"You were wrong to disturb me, my lieutenant. This won't bring you any luck."

"Shut up and give me your name."

"My name is Guérin, Jules Guérin."

"Your regimental number?"

"I don't remember."

"I'll make you remember, I will."

The two non-commissioned officers led the man away, while Horse's Ass grumbled, indignant:

"Ah! He doesn't give a damn about the colonel!"

✼

The next morning, what a scene! On arriving at the station, Anatole found the desk sergeant in a state of the keenest perplexity.

"My lieutenant, who in the world is that civilian you locked up last night? Ah, he made such a racket all night! There, can you hear him yelling?"

Anatole had turned pale.

Damn! If the man wasn't a reservist...

Just then, a corporal brought in the prisoner.

"Ah, it's you, little man," cried the captive, "who had me arrested last night without the hint of a reason! Well, you indulged in a little joke that will cost you dearly!"

Horse's Ass was ashen.

"Aren't you a reservist?"

"So that's it, you mistake me for one of those filthy dogfaces like you! Me, I just came from the *Chass' d'Af'!*"

"You see me in despair, monsieur..."

"You had me arrested illegally, and detained arbitrarily. I will immediately file a complaint with the public prosecutor."

During this exchange, the men had gathered around the station, and an adjutant came to inquire about the cause of the scandal.

Horse's Ass hurriedly whispered into the prisoner's ear a few words that seemed to pacify him.

They both moved off, talking and gesticulating.

After a few minutes, in a small cafe nearby, Horse's Ass drew from his pocket an object that furiously resembled a checkbook, and detached a sheet from it, which he covered with feverish characters, and then returned to the barracks, where he immediately "picked up" a week of confinement, for arriving late to duty.

✼

That very evening, a large group of reservists, after a copious dinner in the best hotel in Lisieux, spent an exquisite evening at the Café Dubois.

We bought champagne for all the little singers, insisting, however, that they drink it with a thousand cries of "Hooray for Horse's Ass!"

That was the least of it!

From that day on, the fearsome Horse's Ass became as mild as a herd of sheep. You could have given him the finger in the middle of the report room and he wouldn't have said a word.

He strictly abstained from frequenting the vesperal areas of Lisieux.

Only, when his twenty-eight days of service were over, when he returned home, and some obsequious employee hastened to greet him with:

"Good day, my lieutenant! How are you, my lieutenant? Did you have a good trip, my lieutenant?"

My lieutenant here, my lieutenant there!

Anatole Duveau exclaimed in a dismal voice:

"The first one to call me 'my lieutenant,' I'll toss him out the door!"

A MALCONTENT[1]

That man on the sidewalk, waiting for the Batignolles-Clichy-Odéon bus, at the same time as me, I was sure that I knew him, but where had I seen him, and what was his name? Cruel enigma!

Although not a young man, he was a man who was still young.

His features, his mannerisms, his entire appearance, indicated someone who was restless, touchy, and ill-tempered.

The bus finally arrived.

As the numbers were called, the crowd surged forward, splashing through the mud that covered Paris, that day, with a fluid and unusually copious mantle.

7, 8, and 9 boarded.

The man who was still young, bearing number 10, grumbled words of disappointment that ended with the cry "Hooray for Boulanger!"

"Well, good," I thought, "a malcontent!"

Another wait, another bus, another splashing.

This time, we were able to climb onto the platform, my provisional stranger and I.

I paid my fare with three bronze centimes.

The man did the same with the help of a two franc coin, upon which the conductor gave him the sum of one franc and seventy centimes, composed entirely of small change.

"What do you expect me to do with all of this grapeshot?" the man cried in exasperation.

---

1. I have insisted on publishing this story, despite its rather stale topicality, to show future generations the attitude of certain French citizens in the years of our grace 1889-1891.

"I'm terribly sorry," the conductor replied, with a courtesy one seldom encounters in that class of functionaries, "but I have no larger coins in my pouch."

Still grumbling, the man distributed his thirty-four sous into different pockets, and emitted a second cry of "Hooray for Boulanger!"

At that moment, he noticed me, recognized me, and shook my hand with all the outward signs of the greatest pleasure.

"I'm sure that you don't recognize me," he said.

"I do, but I don't really remember..."

"I might have guessed. It only happens to me. I recognize all my friends, and none of my friends recognizes me. Hooray for Boulanger!"

He decided to give his name: Fortuné Bidard. I instantly remembered my old school chum.

Fortuné Bidard! If ever a name went poorly with a personality, it was his.

From earliest childhood, life for him had been nothing but a perpetual harvest of misfortunes, a forest of gaffes, a hurricane of undeserved punishment.

Every day was marked by an unfortunate episode befalling Bidard in class, in the street, or in his family.

An excellent student, he never won the smallest prize, and was never awarded the slightest certificate.

It was as if a legion of evil little demons swarmed around Fortuné, plotting to ruin his every move.

One adventure, among others:

One day, we were given a test in mathematics for an important competition. Fortuné worked with concentration, mixed with joy. It was evidently going well.

Suddenly, Bidard mopped his brow, and rubbed his hands in utter satisfaction.

"Are you done?" I asked in a low voice.

"Yes, I just have to copy it out... It's wonderful, my friend, I didn't miss a problem."

Then, before he recopied his paper, he raised his right arm and snapped his fingers. The proctor understood, and agreed.

Bidard's absence was brief.

He hurried back, adjusting his suspenders, returned to his seat, and let out a cry of horror that went straight to our hearts.

Among the papers he had taken, you know where, were the problems he had worked so successfully.

Try to find them now! Of course, there was no time to redo them, and, once again, a pretty prize in mathematics slipped through his fingers.

Unfortunate Fortuné! He told me that luck had continued to give him a cold shoulder with the same persistence.

"Nothing succeeded for me, my poor friend. I worked like a slave, and had all the trouble in the world to pass my exams. And you want me to be content? Bah! Hooray for Boulanger!"

"Hooray for Boulanger!"

"And women, too! More success on my part! I won't tell you about my first experiences with women, it would make your hair stand on end. But recently, I had a little girlfriend, very nice, very sweet, and whom I thought was faithful. Her name was Caroline. One day, I arrived alone at the cafe where we usually went together, Caroline and I. One of my friends asked, "What have you done with Caroline?" I don't know what came over me, but I thought I'd make a joke, so I answered, "Caroline? I dumped her!" At that, he shook my hand and said, "Well, old fellow, congratulations on getting rid of the little slut, who slept with all of your friends, except the ones who weren't interested." I asked around: it was true. And you want me to be content? Bah! Hooray for Boulanger!"

"Hooray for Boulanger!"

"But I must leave you... Just imagine, I'm making my first call on my fiancée, a charming individual, the daughter of a shopkeeper on rue de Richelieu ... I don't know why, but I have a feeling that something will happen between now and then. We're almost there. Here's my stop. Goodbye!"

"Goodbye!"

Fortuné Bidard shook my hand, and went down the steps.

He went further down than he expected, for I saw him flat on the ground, which (as I already told you) was covered with a pretty coat of very thick, very black, and very abundant mud.

Bidard stood up in a rage, and even as the bus arrived at the National Library, I could still hear his cries of "Hooray for Boulanger!"

"Hooray for Boulanger," I echoed, with a note of pity.

THE POSTSCRIPT
OR A VERY OBEDIIENT YOUNG WOMAN

I don't know what you do, when you accompany a friend to the station, after the train has left. I don't know and don't need to know.

As for me, I'm not ashamed to reveal my attitude in those circumstances; I go to the bar in said station and order a Vermouth Cassis (very little cassis) to drown my distress. For, as the poet said: To part is to die a little.

If the time of departure happens not to coincide with that of the aperitif, I order another beverage appropriate for that moment in the day.

So it was that last Tuesday, at the stroke of six thirty in the evening, I found myself seated at the buffet of the Lyon station, before an Absinthe Anisée (very little anisette).

The person I had just accompanied (this detail is none of your business, I offer it in sheer generosity) was a young woman of great beauty, but with such a temper!, that I felt quite relieved to see her depart for other climes.

But no sooner had I wetted my lips with the glaucous liqueur, when a man sat at the table next to mine.

This personage ordered an Amaro Curaçao (very little Curaçao), and pen and paper.

After having satisfied himself that the amaro he was served was truly Michel amaro, and the Curaçao genuine Reischoffen Curaçao, the man took his pen in hand and wrote two letters.

The first, short, effortlessly composed, was soon enclosed in an envelope bearing this address:

Colonel I.-A. du Rabiot
Hôtel des Bains
Pourd-sur-Alaure.

The second letter took more effort than the first.

Some paragraphs flowed from his pen, rapid, concise, ready-made. Other sentences arrived only at the cost of a thousand pains.

Two or three times, he tore the letter into pieces and began again.

At one moment, I saw the poor fellow crush, with the tip of his finger, a tear pearling at his eyelashes.

This man was obviously writing to his loved one. (Will women ever know how much they hurt us?)

Everything comes to an end down here, even love letters. When the four pages were blackened from top to bottom, the man enclosed them, as if with regret, in an envelope on which he had written this address:

Madame Louise du R...
General Delivery
Pourd-sur-Alaure.

"Waiter," he called loudly, "two three sou stamps!"

"Here you are, monsieur," replied the waiter.

Up to that point, the gentleman's features had presented an exterior of completely melancholic dejection.

Suddenly, a flush of rage illuminated his face.

With an angry finger, he tore open the envelope to Madame Louise du R..., and added to the letter a postscript that must have been a corker.

That postscript contained only two lines, but two lines that were, without a doubt, forcibly expressed. — Take that, old girl!

I began to take an interest in this little drama, which was easy to decipher, besides.

The man was obviously the friend of Colonel I.-A. du Rabiot and the lover of the coloneless Louise.

The colonel, him I imagined in the mold of Ramollot, healing his wounds in the waters of Pourd-sur-Alaure.

As for Louise, I was already dumbly in love with her.

"Waiter," I called loudly, "the timetable!"

"Here you are, monsieur," replied the waiter.

There was a train for Pourd-sur-Alaure at 7:40.

Just enough time for a quick bite, and I bought my ticket.

Pourd-sur-Alaure is a little spa, still not very well known, but charming, and situated, as the prospectus says, in marvelous surroundings.

I arrived at about midnight, and had myself taken to the Hôtel des Bains.

I was dreaming of Louise, and the morning seemed long.

Finally, the clock struck for lunch. My heart beat more loudly than the clock: I was going to see Louise, she who merited such tender letters and angry postscripts.

And I saw her.

Little, quite young, quite plump, and so blonde! Not extraordinarily pretty, but as juicy as the devil. Louise abounded in all of my ideals at the time.

She read, while awaiting the colonel, a letter that I recognized. At the postscript, she smiled, a funny little smile, and stuffed the letter in her pocket.

The colonel, limping slightly, arrived in turn.

"I received a note from Alfred," he said.

"Ah!"

"Yes, he had a lot to say."

"Ah!"

And the whole chubby little person of Louise shook with a long burst of silent giggles.

She noticed that I was devouring her with my eyes, and did not seem overly upset.

By dessert, we were the best of friends.

The afternoon only increased our mutual affinity.

Dinner strengthened our bonds.

The evening in the casino was definitive.

At the stroke of ten, she asked me simply:

"What's the number of your hotel room?"

"Seventeen."

"Walk out... In five minutes I'm yours."

After five minutes, she arrived.

"But, your husband...?" I asked timidly.

"Don't worry about my husband, he's playing whist. You know what 'whist' means?"

"Silence."

"Exactly. So, keep quiet and do like me."

In an instant, she shed her finery.

In a second instant, she slipped, a pink serpent, betwixt the white linens.

In a third instant, if you will excuse the expression, she lavished upon me her ultimate favors.

A line of dots, if you please.

.   .   .   .

When we had finished laughing, we chatted.

"And Alfred?" I asked sarcastically.

"So you know Alfred?" she asked, somewhat surprised.

"Not at all, I only know that he wrote you a letter yesterday... especially a postscript!"

"Ah yes, a postscript!... Well, he missed a fine occasion to hold his peace, that one, with his postscript! Would you like to read that postscript of his?"

"Certainly."

This is what the postscript said:

"*P.S. — And besides, in fact, I'm pretty stupid to get so upset over you! Go get f.....!*"

That last word spelled out in full.

"   .   .   .   .   !"

added Louise, in a tone that was frankly cynical, but so amusing!

A NEW BOATING

It had been at least a week since I had seen my old friend Henry Villier-Gauthars. A bit worried, I went up to his place.

Ensconced in an enormous armchair, draped in an ample dressing gown, slumped over, Henry was sipping the contents of an oceanesque bowl of herbal tea (*tilia eoropoea, Linn.*).

"Are you sick, old fellow?" I asked sympathetically.

"I'm feeling better, thank you, but I did well to take care of myself. If not, I'd be in Sainte-Anne today."

"In Sainte-Anne!"

"Yes, my friend, or some other insane asylum."

"Are you joking?"

"Not a whit! Just imagine that on the boulevard des Batignolles... Do you know the boulevard des Batignolles?"

"Like my own pocket."

"Well then, I saw boats passing!"

"Boats? On the boulevard des Batignolles!"

"Yes, old man, boats! Six little boats towed by a little steamboat."

I know the boulevard des Batignolles better than any man. I have explored it in every direction, and have never met the slightest trace of navigation, either by sail or by steam.

Therefore, my friend's mental state seemed to me to be considerably damaged. I asked him to recount his adventure in the minutest detail.

❈

This is it, he said.

One evening last week, as a result of having imbibed billows of fermented drinks and ungaugeable amounts of spirits, I found myself drunk, but, you know, as drunk as a bull in a china shop.

A little woman I met at the Divan Japonais seemed to me the very coalition of all perfections and graces.

She accepted, without fuss, that I share her couch, and off we went, in a car headed in some direction that I didn't even think to notice.

After trying, in vain, to offer some gallant compliments to the lady, I nodded off like the lout that I am.

I awoke in the night, my head heavy, my stomach none too certain, suffering from that phenomenon well known to drinkers, which people of the lower classes call a "hangover" (*pendere supra* would be more scientific).

A bit of air, I thought, would do me good, so I went to the window.

It was as dark as a cave in Haiti.

Where the devil was I?

I thought I recognized a street below, with sidewalks and trees; but I abandoned that idea when I saw six little boats rigged as sloops, towed by a steamboat, whose shape I could not quite distinguish.

"Well!" I said to myself. "It's a canal. But which canal?"

And because I was getting cold, I went back to bed.

It was broad daylight when I awoke a second time.

"Where am I?" I asked the lady.

"But... in my apartment, my little cat."

"Where's that, your apartment?"

"Boulevard des Batignolles."

"So, it's the boulevard des Batignolles we see from your window?"

"Why, yes, my little cat."

"You lie, madame! It's not the boulevard des Batignolles, it's a canal!"

"How so, a canal?"

"Precisely! A canal... I saw boats passing by, last night."

"You were dreaming, my little cat."

"No, I wasn't dreaming, I saw boats."

I dressed and left, not without handsomely remunerating the immodest creature.

It was indeed the boulevard des Batignolles, but then, those boats?...

Because I hadn't been dreaming, do you understand? I hadn't been dreaming! I was sure I'd seen those boats, just as I see you now.

So, I was frightened!

I went to see Charcot, who forbade me alcohol, women, and different other accessories.

I'm trying bromide and hydrotherapy.

I'm feeling better, but it's about time!

If I hadn't taken care of myself, today I might be watching Admiral Gervais's squadron sailing down the Stevens passage.

❋

Poor Villier-Gauthars!

I thought that a little distraction would do him good, so I convinced him to accompany me to a fair in a location near Paris, whose name I could not possibly reveal (without being an utter cad).

We visited the beautiful Férid'jé, we slid down the roller coaster, we trembled at Bidel's menagerie; in short, we were well on our way to draining the cup of fairground delights, when, suddenly, Villier-Gauthars raised his arms to the heavens.

"Oh no," I thought, "a fit!"

"My God!" he shouted. "The boats! The boats!"

"All right, all right, calm down."

"The boats! There are the boats I saw on the boulevard des Batignolles!"

"Calm down, my poor friend, calm down!"

"My God, my God! What an idiot I am! What an idiot I am!"

And it was impossible to get anything out of him except "What an idiot I am! What an idiot I am!"

After a few minutes of epileptiform laughter, he indicated the attraction known under the name of "Sea on Land," which is composed of little boats driven and shaken circularly by steam power. Everyone can enjoy, for a derisive sum, the charming sensation of pitching and rolling.

To travel from one fairground to another, the owner of this attraction hitches his boats to his car (built in the form of a steam-carriage).

Those were the boats that Villier-Gauthars had seen on the boulevard des Batignolles, during a night of debauchery.

✸

Now, he was completely cured.

"What an idiot I am!" he repeated one more time.

"A bock, eh?"

"Gladly."

The bock was followed by innumerable other drinks.

And at each glass, as if in excuse, my friend said:

"That bromide made me so damn thirsty!!!"

THE LANGUAGE OF FLOWERS

I will admit that, possibly, a tourist who had spent a century or two away from someplace might not be overly surprised to find, on his return, rubble and ruin where he had once contemplated sumptuous palaces; but such was not my case.

After an absence of five or six months, I was not a little stunned to encounter, at one of the places on the coast most familiar to me, a manor in full decrepitude, an old feudal manor that I was quite sure I had not encountered the year before, neither there nor anywhere.

My detective's intuition led me to suspect that the ruins were artificial, and probably of recent date.

The castle in question presented, besides, an appearance far more ludicrous than sinister; everything stank of the fake: chipped crenelations, dismantled towers, misfired machicolations, ogival windows studded with bars whose thickness would have challenged the most powerful barometers; it was completely idiotic. A few inquiries in the countryside quickly informed me about the history of this neo-old construction and its proprietor.

A former chiropodist to the Queen of Romania, Baron Lagourde, who is a baron about as much as I am an archimandrite, had accumulated an immense fortune in the exercise of his delicate functions.

(For, at the risk of irritating certain lyrical imaginations, I will conceal from you no longer the fact that Carmen Sylva, much like you and I, finds herself at the head of feet with several corns, and that the guard who watches the barriers of the Louvre does not turn away queens.)

Baron Lagourde (we'll let him keep the title, since it seems to give him pleasure) is a common fat man, ugly, vain, and as stupid as his feet, which are enormous.

His wife, whom he brought back from Western Bulgaria, presents the appearance of a dark little woman, unkempt but extraordinarily adulterous. This Bulgar of the West (or Bulgar Saint-Lazare, as we usually say in Paris) cheated on her husband, in effect, with a never-ending stream, if you will excuse the expression, of roadmen.

Why roadmen, you may ask, rather than rural postmen or embassy attachés? Mysteries of the feminine heart!

The baroness adored roadmen, and let them know it. That is why the road between Trouville and Honfleur was so badly kept, that summer, while they were kept so well.

Baron Lagourde settled in the area last year; he bought an admirably situated property, from which one saw a superb panorama: to the right, the bay of the Seine; in front, the harbor of Le Havre; to the west, the open sea.

Without losing an instant, the former royal chiropodist redesigned his new acquisition according to his esthetic and to his feudal tastes.

In no time at all, the manor arose from the ground; special workmen gave it that antiquey cachet without which nothing can be seriously feudal. To complete the illusion, real skeletons loaded with chains were tossed gaily into the dungeons.

The baron would have been the happiest of men in his imitation Middle Ages but for the stubbornness of old man Fabrice. One could even say, without fear of being accused of exaggeration, that old man Fabrice was "ornery."

The object of dispute was a nearby field, not very wide, but very long, which dominated the baron's feudalism, and from which one had an even more splendid view, a field that might have been worth about six hundred francs in legal tender.

Lagourde offered 1000 francs for it, then 1100, and finally, from offer to offer, 2000 francs.

"It's worth more than that, Baron, it's worth more than that," jeered the shrewd old man, shaking his head.

But that sum of 2000 francs was the limit of the baron's concessions, and he said no more on the subject.

One day that summer, the lordly chiropodist, having ascended one of his towers, explored the horizon with the aid of his excellent Flammarion binoculars.

Right by the coast, a yacht chugged leisurely along: on deck, ladies and gentlemen were focusing binoculars themselves, and appeared overcome with Homeric gaiety. They passed the binoculars to one another, and doubled over scandalously.

Baron Lagourde felt slightly offended. Was it his manor they were mocking like that?

The next day, at the same time, the same yacht returned, accompanied, this time, by two pleasure boats, whose passengers manifested, as on the day before, exuberant high spirits.

On all of the following days, the same business.

Entire flotillas came, slackening their pace as soon as the castle came into view. On board, the passengers seemed to enjoy ineffable pleasures.

The fishermen of Trouville, of Villerville, of Honfleur, no longer passed without noisy amusement.

In short, all of the local nautical society, from the opulent Ephrussi to my scraphappy friend Baudry, known as "The Temper," had great fun for several weeks, like a whole asylum of little lunatics.

Very worried, very annoyed, very tormented, the baron resolved to set his mind at ease, and to see for himself the reason for this derogatory hilarity.

One fine morning, he chartered a boat, and set sail for the spot that seemed to afford everyone such pleasure.

After he had sailed for a quarter of an hour, his manor appeared, more feudal than ever, and not a bit ludicrous. So what were they laughing at, all those imbeciles!

Sudden horror! The baron could not believe his eyes! Anger, indignation, and a host of other fierce sentiments empurpled his features. He had just seen... Was it possible?

Beneath his manor, and fully visible, old man Fabrice's field spread out in the sun like an immense green banner, a banner on which was written a yellow inscription, and that inscription bore these terrifyingly legible words:

BARON LAGOURDE IS A CUCKOLD!

The miracle was quite simple: that old rascal Fabrice had planted his field with little yellow flowerets called buttercups, arranging them into a graphic pattern to produce that outrageous and precise meaning: old man Fabrice had practiced anthography on a vast scale.

Baron Lagourde sat in the boat, dazed with shame and bewilderment before the terrible sentence that shone out so gaily in bright yellow against the dark green field.

"Baron Lagourde is a cuckold! Baron Lagourde is a cuckold!" he repeated, completely stunned.

The laughter of the men accompanying him brought him back to reality.

"Take me back to land!" he commanded, in the most feudal tone he could muster.

He went straight to the mayor.

"Your Honor," he said, "I am insulted in the most serious terms on the territory of your commune. It is your duty to see that I am respected, and I hope you will act accordingly."

"Insulted, Baron? And how?"

"A certain scoundrel, old man Fabrice, has dared to write on his field that I am a cuckold!"

"How's that? On his field?"

"Exactly, with yellow flowers."

Fortunately, the mayor had long been aware of old man Fabrice's excellent joke, for he would have understood none of the baron's explanations.

The two men went to see the defamer, who welcomed them with astonished good grace:

"Me, Baron! Me, I would have dared to write that the baron is a cuckold! Ah, I am greatly pained that the baron thinks me capable of such a thing!"

"Let's go to the site," said the mayor.

On the site, they could see green grass and yellow flowers arranged in a certain way, but they were unable, despite the very best of intentions, to make any sense of the pattern. They were too close.

(This phenomenon is analogous to the one that makes certain flies wander, for entire lifetimes, across *in quartos* without understanding a single word of the simplest texts.)

"The baron knows quite well," continued old man Fabrice, "that wildflowers, they grow pretty much where they want. If I'm to be blamed for that!..."

"And you, Your Honor," grumbled the baron, "is that your opinion as well?"

"My God, Baron, I certainly want to believe that you're insulted, because you say you are; but, in any case, it's not on the territory of my commune, because the inscription is not legible. You are insulted on the sea... complain to the Secretary of the Navy."

The baron did better than complain to the Secretary of the Navy, which would have entailed some delay.

"All right, you old crook," he said to old man Fabrice, "how much for your field"

"The baron knows quite well that I don't want to sell it, but because the baron likes it so much, I will let him have it for ten thousand francs, and the baron can boast of getting a good deal. A field where flowers write things by themselves!"

That very evening, old man Fabrice's attempt at anthography perished under the gardener's pitiless scythe.

Now, if I had some advice to give Baron Lagourde, I would suggest that he not use the same method to play a joke on old man Fabrice, next year.

Old man Fabrice has infinite contempt for the opinion of his fellow citizens.

BÉBERT

The little restaurant where, in those days, I ate my lunch (a humble meal whose price, seldom less than ninety centimes, never surpassed twenty-two sous), recruited its most shining clientele from the perfumers across the street. A clientele that was sober as well, but oh how aromatic! And so diversely!

Some days, it was the unappetizing ylang-ylang that dominated; other days, the cephalalgic wintergreen.

Or else you thought yourself lost in infinite harvests of geraniums, violets, or tuberoses. It all gave the fries a funny smell.

But what did fragrance matter, to our appetites at twenty, for whom lunch is the best meal of the day, and dinner too.

And besides, why should roses disgust us with sausages?

All those little perfumers were as pretty as they smelled good.

One, especially!

One no bigger than that! And a redhead, but, you know, a redhead to the point of indecency.

Oh, little redhead, you will never know I loved you at first sight, and how greedily I contemplated your neck, where your fine golden fleece went to die, down there, in mad curls!

So white her skin, that no whiter was ever seen.

So black her eyes, that no blacker were ever seen.

Two carbuncles in a bowl of milk, as Chincholle would say.

Somewhat large, her mouth, but furnished so sumptuously!

And besides, I have always adored somewhat large mouths on little redheads.

With all that, a mischievous air and funny words.

She sang all the time.

And I think they were hers, those little refrains, because I never heard them anywhere else, neither the words nor the music, which were deliciously stupid, as well.

She left every evening at seven.

I waited for her, and walked with her a little way.

"Well, good evening," she said, at the Place du Châtelet. "Go home now, that's better than saying silly things."

"Good evening."

And I went away dutifully, but I would have much preferred to say silly things.

And do them.

One day, she told me she had a little boyfriend, a certain Bébert.

It was foolish, but I was terribly annoyed, and swore the most sanguinary hatred for this Bébert.

A little Bébert of no importance, she told me, but she loved him all the same.

And with rage in my heart, my voice bitter, I asked every day, with respectful sarcasm, after Bébert's health.

"And now go home, that's better than saying silly things."

One evening, one Saturday evening, she did not throw it in my face, that mocking and disappointing phrase.

That evening, I shall always remember, she smelled of verbena, with a faint scent of mown hay.

Her arm rested on mine.

I crossed the Pont-au-Change, in a dream, the boulevard du Palais in a delirium. To cross the Saint-Michel bridge, my feet sprouted wings. On the journey along the boulevard Saint-Michel, all notion of reality had deserted my brain.

I traveled into the beyond, up there, by the Observatory.

We dined at my place.

After the coffee, she put her white paw in my hand, and said, in a languid and husky voice I had never heard from her:

"Why don't we take a walk in the Luxembourg Gardens... *before*."

"Before"!

It was a declaration!

For, during dinner, we had talked about nothing in particular.

I repeated that delicious word: "before"!

And in vain did I cling to reality, I could scarcely believe my luck.

Well, since there was a "before," there would be an "after," and especially a "during"!

We took a walk in the Gardens, "before."

And, immediately "after," I had at my complete disposition her pretty white liliaceous body.

Liliaceous! Don't laugh, you can believe me.

Her pretty little body, as white as the Flower of France, and equally pure and immaculate!

The next morning, she left my domicile, like a young mouse raised by an old eel.

I didn't hear her go.

On Monday, her companions informed me that she was not returning to the store.

Unknown her residence, unknown her new address.

It was only after a long year that I saw her again.

"How you hurt me!" I sobbed.

She looked at me as if trying to remember me.

Then she burst out laughing:

"Oh, yes! It's you!" she said.

And she told me that, having become a milliner, she was completely with Bébert now, and very happy.

I offered bitter and tender reproaches.

"What," she cried, "you poor fool..."

And, at that moment, she glared at me from the top of her little height, with infinite contempt:

"What, you poor fool, don't you understand that if I went home with you, it was only to spare Bébert an unpleasant chore!"

Ever since, whenever I meet little redheads on the street who smell like verbena, I don't know what stops me from slapping them.

MIOUSIC

(In C, 3/4) So la do, ti la ti mi.

BERNICAT

That year, that is, in 18.. (which doesn't make me any younger), on Christmas Eve, our celebrations had surpassed the ordinary limitations of a normal Christmas Eve.

I'm not referring to the conduct of the guests, which was faultless, but to the duration of the festivities.

The blue of the morning, in fact, had long since rubbed its gum eraser over the gold of the stars, and we were still at the table.

Each guest, hugging close his guestess, broached in turn the highest summits of esthetics, and the no less formidable social questions.

Without hesitation, whole groups of us sliced the most intractable Gordian knots, and if, that morning, we had been the government...!

My guestess, mine, was a ravishing plump blonde, silly, sentimental, light pink, a good little shopgirl.

Lucie was her name.

Her eyes (oh, her eyes!), as limpid as those of a little child, her mouth (oh, her mouth), which seemed plucked, that very morning, from the most royal cherry tree in Montmorency, her blonde hair (such a color!), very fine, in a multitude that verged on indiscretion, her hands (oh, her hands!) composed solely of dimples; everything about her, everything, complicated by a copious preliminary extra-dry, put me into a state whose most chaste description would get me hauled before my country's judiciary.

She laughed at the stupid things I said.

She laughed with a pretty idiotic laugh that crowned my delight.

My right arm had entwined her waist, my left hand held (easily) her two hands, and my lips gave the fine hair at the nape of her neck a billion kisses, followed immediately by another billion.

Long shivers ran down her back, and she kept laughing, saying no, stupidly.

Suddenly, music arose from the courtyard.

A matutinal barrel organ was playing the famous waltz from *Francis Bluestocking*: "A Hope for Happy Days"... which was, in those days, at the height of its popularity.

Then, Lucie stopped laughing.

It was she who gripped my hand, all troubled, murmuring:

"Oh, that music! That music! I'm dying...!"

I thought for my part that she'd chosen a funny moment for her demise.

Indigestion, maybe? No, simply ecstasy.

"I'm dying," she continued, "and I love you!"

The agony was sweet, and Lucie did not die.

Nor did I.

We were supposed to see each other the following Sunday: she did not come to the rendezvous.

A letter, in which sentimentality precluded orthography, informed me confusedly that she regretted her "mistake" and wished she were dead. (Again?)

I left Paris the next day, summoned to Reykjavik to embalm a Danish professor of toxicology, dead after a fall from a horse.

(Those little Icelandic horses are extremely difficult to mount if one is not used to them.)

❋

Nothing is funnier than things.

One day, I was crossing the rue Grenéta, thinking of Lucie, when I met — you'll never guess in a million years — when I met Lucie.

Lucie!

And I was not back to square one hundred.

I was not back to square fifty.

I was not back to square twenty.

(I will abridge so as not to tire the reader.)

I was not back to square ten.

I was not back to square five.

No, ladies; no, gentlemen, I was not even back to square two.

Believe it or not: I was back...

I was back to square one!

Lucie!

Lucie, a little fatter, adorable to the point of damnation (but what's the risk?); Lucie, more blonde and light pink than ever; Lucie, whose eyes still reflected the limpid innocence of youth.

With the effrontery inherent to her sex, Lucie claimed that she "didn't remember anything."

"And this melody," I said, with a flash of inspiration. "Do you remember this?"

And I hummed the famous waltz: "A Hope for Happy Days."

She seized my hand.

"Stop it, you wretched man! When I hear that melody, I'm ready to love you again, like that Christmas morning, and my eyes automatically search for you."

"And when you don't hear it?"

"I love my husband, monsieur."

"You're married?"

"Yes, monsieur, to a traveling salesman."

"Who travels?"

"Eight months of the year."

"Poor thing!"

"But I must leave you, because this is my neighborhood, and if anyone saw me...!"

Quite caddishly, I followed her, and learned her name, her address.

Soon after, I heard that her husband had left for Roumelia.

❄

One fine morning, I rang at Lucie's door.

She herself answered.

"You, monsieur!"

And she was ready to slam the door in my face without further ado, when, suddenly, there arose from the courtyard the suggestive melody "A Hope for Happy Days."

(Need I inform the reader that the organ in question had been brought there by myself, diabolically?)

Lucie, all at once, melted into the tenderest ecstasy.

She held out her arms to me, whispering two simple words: "Come in."

If I told you that I made her beg me, you wouldn't believe me, and you'd be right: I "went in."

And I went back the next day, and the days after that, always accompanied by my old organ grinder.

Unfortunately, a few difficulties arose!

The other tenants, charmed at first by Lucie's melody, had tossed sous to the fellow.

But, as the famous waltz repeated every day with monotonous insistence, those fine people grew to dislike it, and replaced the sous with less remunerative projectiles, like cabbage stalks, ashes, and other domestic refuse.

I gave the concierge fabulous sums to acquire his neutrality.

Fortunately, Lucie's husband returned about then.

Weary of traveling, he set up his own business.

It was about time!

Lucie never tired of "A Hope for Happy Days": it inspired her.

As for myself, I finally became heartily sick of the wretched tune, and now, it takes the wind from my sails, if you will excuse the expression.

THE PROFITABLE ABSENCE

"All right, she's in no hurry to get home tonight!"

Having thus formulated his despair, the poor man returned his watch to his pocket, useless operation, for, a minute later, he drew it out again, checked the late hour again, and repeated for a change:

"All right, she's in no hurry to get home tonight!"

The fact is that eight o'clock had just rung from all the neighborhood belfries. The soup set on the table, after having briefly verged on ebullition, cooled slowly, but surely, toward the ambient temperature, which was, that evening, if it's of any interest to you, 21 and a fraction degrees centigrade, an acceptable temperature for a cold bouillon, but completely insufficient for any self-respecting hot soup.

And the poor man, with touching stubbornness, drew out his watch, put it back, and murmured, more and more defeated:

"All right, she's in no hurry to get home tonight!"

Who was all right? I couldn't tell you (a figure of speech, probably), but I can inform you about the person who was in no hurry to get home that night: it was his wife, his good little wife.

They had been married a year.

A year! How quickly it passes, all the same! I seem to see her again in the sacristy, in her white dress, with her orange blossom that looked stunned to find itself there, her brown hair in her eyes, her little nose in the air, her mouth that was a bit mischievous, but so funny.

As they left the church, the old ladies of the neighborhood called her a "brazen hussy." Jealous!

Much less appealing was her husband. Pants that were too short compensated, fortunately, for a frock coat that was too long. His shoes, which seemed destined for the long term, made up for his hat brim, which was invisible to the naked eye. In short, an outfit devoid of elegance, but worn so badly!

They had become engaged under strange circumstances.

Our friend Constant Lejaune, a young man of forty-two, employed at the "General Company for Insurance Against the Notaries of France," had long lived in the same building.

This building had a concierge, Madame Ary-Golade, a good fine woman, hooray, who had a daughter, Hélène, who was all of eighteen springs.

Constant took no notice of Hélène's springs. He saw her as no bigger than that, spoke to her, tapped her cheeks, thought she was nice, and that was all.

One evening, Constant, returning from his duties, called gaily to the concierge his habitual:

"Good evening, Madame Alary, no letters for me?"

"No, Monsieur Lejaune, no letters for you; but I have something important to tell you."

Constant entered her lodge, and there received the most dreadful revelation that has ever shaken the soul of a Lejaune. Hélène was in love with him, but madly in love.

Constant was thunderstruck.

Six weeks later, in a room smelling of fresh paint, a deputy mayor of the seventeenth arrondissement declared united in the name of the law Monsieur Constant Lejaune and Mademoiselle Ary-Golade.

The same day, a venerable ecclesiastic from Sainte-Marie des Batignolles blessed the young people's union and exhorted them (and was it any of his business?) to multiply.

Very wrongly, in my opinion, the Lejaune couple moved.

To have the opportunity to combine under the same and solitary head the two glorious titles of concierge and mother-in-law, and to miss that unique opportunity!

Constant, let me tell you in all frankness: you committed, that day, a serious error.

Despite this inconceivable gaffe, the new couple enjoyed unmitigated happiness; or, if mitigation occurred, it only increased their happiness.

Hélène, my God! was no more perfect than another. She was pretty, and unfailingly inspired bundles of covetous looks to converge on her little person.

At first, Constant would have liked her to be indignant. On the contrary, she was delighted. Constant quickly became used to this state of things.

Another of Hélène's imperfections: always late.

If punctuality is, as is said, the politeness of kings, I strongly advise Hélène never to mount a throne, for she would soon earn herself, in foreign courts, a reputation for imperial boorishness.

Fortunately, as far as foreign courts were concerned, Hélène was only acquainted with those on the rue Legendre, where she had spent the brightest years of her tumultuous childhood.

She often happened to return at improbable hours. Let us hasten to add that she was always equipped with excellent excuses. One night, it was because of this, another night it was because of that.

One time, she even stayed out all night!

After a night of torture and anguish for Constant, she returned in the morning, at about nine, rather tired, but filled with satisfaction for a duty accomplished. She had spent the night looking after her aunt in Le Vésinet, who had almost died, the poor woman.

(An aunt whom, parenthetically, Constant had never heard of, but Hélène's aunts were so numerous and so widely distributed that he could have easily forgotten one, in the list.)

Keenly observant, and even a little superstitious, the good man had noticed that each of Hélène's late returns coincided with an administrative favor for him.

One night, Hélène returned at half past midnight; the next morning, the office manager said to Constant, in extremely friendly tones:

"But, my dear Lejaune, you're in a draft. Move to the corner of the office, you'll be more comfortable there."

And always, always the same coincidence! The strange part is that the later Hélène was, the more precious the favor. So, forty-eight hours after that night with the aunt in Le Vésinet, he was promoted to chief clerk.

.　.　.　.　.　.　.　.　.　.　.　.　.　.　.　.　.　.

"All right," murmured Lejaune for the thousand and first time, "she's in no hurry to get home tonight!"

Ding!... It's the concierge, bringing up a letter. Well, a letter from Hélène!

"My idolized darling,

"You know I haven't been feeling very well these days. I went to see a great doctor, who ordered me to take the waters. I was just in time, apparently; another day, and I would have been lost.

"Don't get too bored, my big old sweetheart, and think now and then about the one who will only think of you.

"Your pretty little baby,
"HÉLÈNE.

"PS. — I'll be back in a week."

Constant Lejaune's face, at first upset, suddenly brightened.

"Gone for a week!" he cried. "I'm a cinch to be named manager!"

EXTRA STORIES

BY ANALOGY

A summer story

PROLOGUE

It was in those blessed hours when I was still a student.

Pray unto God, O families, that your sons be more studious than me, and less debauched.

From my years of study, I have kept no glorious memento, no prize, no congratulation from my teachers.

Oh! The interminable loiterer that I was, in Luxembourg, on the docks, on — on sunny days — the terraces of brasseries.

I don't say that to boast, for I know full well that it's very wrong to act that way.

I shattered my future some fifteen times. Said future thus acquired all the flexibility of a very young clown.

And besides, since the future is only separated from the past by the present, and the present does not exist... then what?

Finally, to be honest, I went to the cafe, and spent in that evil place many an evening that would have been more fruitfully occupied with studies that were arid at the time, but subsequently remunerative.

Among my usual comrades, two stood out, who might have been called the antipodes of commotion.

One, Georges Caron; the other, Victor Ducreux.

Georges Caron, as noisy as a cauldron of devils boiling in holy water, deafened us with his idle observations, repeatedly infinitely in a malevolent falsetto.

Victor Ducreux evoked the idea of a carefully padded sepulcher. Never a word, except, in desperate cases, a brief and muffled blasphemy.

Now, this is what happened one day:

I

Or rather one evening.

We had all gathered in the back of a little cabaret on the rue Monsieur-le-Prince, called the Cuckoo, and which the wrecker's pickaxe has since demolished.

Another corner of old Paris... etc....

Why did Georges Caron keep quiet at that moment, and for several moments, and for several moments after?

Be that as it may, this silence abnormalized us so very much, that, with one accord, we shouted out:

"Hey! Caron is gone!"

II

At the same moment — will we ever know why? — the sepulchral Ducreux began chattering, chattering: like a brood of young one-eyed magpies.

Abuse of fermented drink? Or was it some other cerebral overstimulation?

Be that as it may, this noisiness abnormalized us so very much, that, with one accord, we shouted out:

"Hey! Ducreux is gone!"

III

(As I warned you above, this is a summer story.)

PRETTY POLLY

To Séverine

Poor devil!

I can still see him arriving in the morning, gaunt, pale, enveloped in the thin and shiny frock coat of an impoverished professor.

Since he was very gentle and very sad, his students — I among them — found him extremely ridiculous, and never lost a chance to make him unhappy, like the good little bourgeois that we already were, cowardly and cruel.

Heavens! How cold it was that year!

And, despite the rain, the wind, the snow, our professor arrived dressed simply in his thin and shiny frock coat, with the collar turned up.

However, when he returned after the New Year vacation, the poor devil entered class that morning enveloped in an overcoat...

No, my friends, an overcoat!...

The joy that we felt at the sight of that garment reached epileptiform delirium.

And we didn't know which to admire more in that masterpiece, its shape or its color.

Unspeakable, its shape! Badly cut, wrinkling here, pulling there, sticking up behind the neck. And the sleeves! And the pockets! And the buttons!

But what amused us the most was its color.

Imagine that, in the virgin forest of Brazil, you killed a great quantity of parrots, among the greenest parrots in Brazil, and that you wove a fabric from their plumage, and you can picture the color of that famous overcoat.

Immediately, we baptized our professor Pretty Polly, and one witty kid in class cried out "Polly want a cracker?" in the most comical way.

Poor Pretty Polly became even sadder than usual, and two tears seemed to pearl at his eyes.

The famous overcoat amused us for a full week, and then, one fine morning, Pretty Polly, no doubt disgusted with his "threads," showed up before us dressed simply in his thin and shiny frock coat.

And yet, my word! There was one hell of a storm that day.

The next day, no Pretty Polly.

The principal announced to us that our professor, having lost his mother, would be replaced by a teaching assistant for two days.

Pretty Polly returned to us, after the two days, paler, gaunter, sadder, and gentler than before.

Faced with the poor devil's desolation, we could only disarm. We shot fewer spitballs in his face.

Some time after that, one Thursday, I was rummaging through a second-hand shop, looking for dirty books, when I saw in the back of the store, guess what?

Hanging with other used clothes, Pretty Polly's overcoat shone forth in all the glory of its brilliant green.

The opportunity was too good, really.

"How much for the overcoat?"

"Twelve francs."

After long haggling, I obtained a notable discount and, for six francs, the masterpiece became my property.

I had a great deal of trouble obtaining the six francs, I sold a few books, I extorted a small sum from my sister by intimidation, and I believe I took the rest from the paternal cashbox.

The next day, the better to savor my triumph, draped in my green acquisition, I arrived to class somewhat late.

No human pen could depict my indescribable triumph.

My comrades lifted their eyes, saw me, and there was a tremendous and inextinguishable outburst of laughter.

I, with the most natural air in the world, went to my seat.

Pretty Polly, frighteningly pale, had arisen.

"Monsieur," he cried, "you have my overcoat!"

"Not at all, monsieur, it's mine. I bought it yesterday from old lady Polydore."

"Bring it here, I confiscate it."

"No, monsieur, I will not. You have no right to confiscate my belongings."

The discussion became heated. Pretty Polly ordered me to leave. I complained to the principal, who agreed with me.

That evening, I met the poor devil on the street. He called me over, and this is what he said:

"I was wrong to raise my voice this morning. The overcoat is yours because you paid for it. But if you would be considerate, please don't wear it to school, it's too painful for me... You know that I lost my mother the other day. Well, she's the one who made it for me. She found a remnant on sale, and she cut and sewed it herself. When she gave it to me as a New Year's present, the good woman said, "Here, my poor boy, here's a coat, it's not very handsome, but it will keep you warm." Two or three days later, she fell ill... We're not rich; our meager resources were quickly exhausted, and, one fine day, I had to sell the overcoat to buy some wood. Oh! I didn't get much for it... And then, some time later, my mother died. So, you understand, when you make fun of my green overcoat, it seems to me that you're making fun of my poor mother, and it's very painful to me."

And at that moment, he looked at me; I was weeping like a dumb animal.

I begged his forgiveness, and that very evening, insisted on giving him back his relic, which I no longer found ridiculous.

And, ever since then, when I see coats that are badly cut, with funny sleeves, and funny pockets, I think that some poor old mother might have spent the night sewing it, and said in the morning, "Here, my boy, it's not very handsome, but it will keep you warm."

And I don't laugh.

DELICACY

The guano is a beautiful bird.
WILLY.

Well! Yes, that's right, I'm getting married.

A stupid idea, you say? I know it as well as you.

One doesn't marry those women, you say? You can see very well that one does, since I'm marrying one.

I'd like to see you in my place, you who say such things. And it's all the fault of the mud.

What a funny thing it is, the mud in Paris!

In the country, yes, I understand why there's mud. The rain mixes with the earth, and there you have it.

But in Paris? The rain doesn't mix with the cobblestones, or the asphalt. So, what then?

When I become immensely rich (in the first week of February), I will offer a prize of three hundred fifty thousand francs for the best work on "Parisian Mud Through the Ages."

I say "Parisian mud," but I could say "muds," because there are as many kinds as there are streets in the capital.

All things being equal, then, depending on the neighborhood, there are hard muds, there are liquid muds, there are black muds, there are gray muds. I have even see violet. (I must add that it was in a painting by Henri Rivière.)

One mud that I can particularly recommend to you, is the mud on the rue des Martyrs.

It's like cold cream in mourning.

Soft, unctuous, lubricating, it could be prescribed by our most prominent physicians for chilblains, or sore and cracked nipples.

It reminds me, although darker, of "degras."

Did they use degras, in your regiment?

In ours, the 119th, all the men were ordered to coat their shoes with degras once a week.

This product has no equal for maintaining and softening leather. We even had a captain who claimed that it *nourished* it.

Some food!

Except, the day after the degras, we always had a devil of a time shining our boots.

Every time I mention degras, I laugh myself to tears, at an excellent joke I played on a young man who had joined the regiment that very day.

He tasted his rations melancholically.

"What's the matter, old man, not hungry?"

"Not much... I don't like beef."

"Why don't you put some mustard on it? It will go down easier."

"Mustard? I'd like some... Where is it?"

Obligingly, I brought him the pot of degras.

The poor fellow, unsuspectingly, accepted an ample portion of that product on the cover of his mess tin, and dipped a bite of his "meat" abundantly into it.

Me, I was literally doubled over in my bed.

The funniest part of the story, is that the young man, while making terrible attempts to vomit, broke something in his stomach and died that night, in the hospital.[1]

I never laughed so hard.

.   .   .   .

Unctuosity, a quality appreciated in cold cream and prelates (have you noticed how unctuous prelates are?) constitutes for the mud on the rue des Martys a formidable attribute.

---

[1]. This case, of great interest, elucidates a very controversial point in medical legislation, that is, that ingestion, into the system, of even a non-toxic substance, can be ruled a cause of death. (Translator's note.)

It makes the pavement slippery.

And that is exactly what I was coming to.

The other night, I was returning home.

It had rained all day.

The ground had become so lubricated, that everyone was walking with infinite precautions, like sailors on a bowsprit coated with soft soap.

Until that moment, the axis of my body had maintained itself in relative verticality. When I reached the Cafe des Martys, bang!, my feet slipped, and I tumbled onto the asphalt of the sidewalk.

Ah! How clean I was!

Confused, ashamed, ridiculous, I lost my head in the middle of a crowd that was greatly amused by my misadventure, when I felt a tug at my sleeve.

A little blonde who said, "Come with me, I'll brush you off."

She lived across the street.

At times like that, you don't try to be clever: I accepted.

The little blonde stripped me of my garments, dried them, brushed them with fully maternal care, and restored their reputation.

During this time, I examined the premises, with a scrutinizing eye.

Without a doubt, I had found myself in the room of a merchant of love.

I thought there was no better way to express my gratitude than to offer myself as a customer... immediately.

But she gently disengaged herself from my embrace, murmuring, "No... No... I don't want to."

"But why don't you want to?"

"Because!"

"Because why?"

"Because you'll say that's why I offered to brush your clothes."

It was absurd, but she wouldn't change her mind, that little blonde.

The most irritating part, is that she was very nice.

I went back the next day.

She still refused my advances, with her eternal: "No, I don't want to... You'll say that's why I offered to brush your clothes."

"But I assure you I won't say that!"

"You'll think it, it's the same thing."

I went back every day, and every day met the most pitiless refusals.

This delicacy touched me, and, before two weeks, that little blonde will become the mother of my children.

THE PARISH PRIEST

To Leo XIII.

My long association with ecclesiastics permits me to speak with some authority about the various reasons that convince young men to become priests.

Some, rarer and rarer, alas! throw themselves into the priesthood from pure religious vocation.

Others, lazy sons of farmers, contemplating with terror the harsh existence of the fields and the monotonous menu in the cottages, acquire early on a pronounced taste for the pampered and rolling-in-cloverish life of a country priest.

Certain others, unworthy of the glorious name of Frenchmen, feel an instinctive horror for spilled blood, especially their own, preferring the canons of the church to the cannons of Colonel de Bange.

A fourth category consists of young men who, barely out of adolescence, hold this highly philosophical discussion with themselves:

"Let's see... What should I do with my life?... Ah, an idea!... What if I became a priest... There's a job where you don't get bored."

And I don't find that so ridiculous.

It is this last series that claims my excellent friend, Father Chamel, the abbott of Ventrouilly (Yonne-Inférieur).

Last summer, I was invited to spend a few days at the castle of Ventrouilly.

On the day that I arrived, walking through the countryside, I heard the sound of a guitar coming from a pretty little house at the back of a garden.

I adore the guitar, especially when played well, which was the case.

A farmer was walking by:

"Could you tell me, my good man, who it is that plays the guitar so well?"

"Why, yes, monsieur," the obliging Burgundian replied, "that's our parish priest."

A priest who plays the guitar, that's odd.

That evening, leafing through an album, I discovered some watercolor landscapes:

"Well!" I said. "These aren't too badly daubed... Who painted them?"

"It was our parish priest."

A priest who paints watercolors, that's odd.

And then, all the time, our parish priest.

Our parish priest here, our parish priest there.

A mighty fisherman before the Lord, nobody but that parish priest could catch trout that weighed I don't know how many pounds, and even kilos.

A tall lad, rather stocky, the parish priest didn't look the least bit sacerdotal.

On Sundays, when, chalice in hand, he changed the chablis into the blood of Christ, he looked to me like someone in a costume, fooling around with his vermouth.

The parish priest was much loved at the castle, in those days.

Now, they're a bit cooler, but it won't last, I hope. The parish priest is so nice.

One morning, I was walking in the park, trying to find a rhyme for "investigation," when the guard passed, shouldering his rifle.

"Good morning, Pascal," I said, "fine weather, this morning."

"Good morning, Monsieur Eugène... Why yes, fine weather... It will be hot today."

"Where are you going like that, Pascal?"

"To take a little walk in the woods, and see if there's anything new."

And I went off with Pascal to see if there was anything new in the woods.

There was nothing new, but there was a boar going by.

Pascal fired a bullet in the general area of its neck.

(I apologize to my readers for telling them this cynegetic fact in such bourgeois terms. I am the unluckiest hunter in the kingdom, and lack the authoritative pen of M. Jules Roques, master of the hounds.)

The boar was hit, for he let out a terrible grunt and vanished wildly into the underbrush.

"We have him," said Pascal. "He can't go far."

And following the trail of blood, we tried to catch up to him.

Unfortunately, the forest is very thick in that part, and we had to walk slowly.

The trail of blood led us to the ditch that borders the road.

Then, nothing.

Not a trace, neither blood nor tracks.

Had the boar burrowed into the ground, like a mole?

Had some giant lammergeier carried it off in its talons?

Or had it simply evaporated into the atmosphere, like a drop of ether?

Mystery! Cruel enigma!

All we knew, was that there was no more boar there than in our hands.

Pascal cursed between his teeth, and declared it was more surprising than a bolt from the blue dropping a bombshell when you least expected it.

Not long afterward, we learned the answer to the riddle.

The parish priest was returning in a car from a nearby village, with a choirboy.

Just as he was crossing the woods, he spotted the boar, which had just collapsed into the ditch, completely exhausted.

To jump to the ground, finish off the animal with a slash of his knife, and hoist it into the car, was all, for Father Chamel, but the work of an instant.

And then, off we go, mum's the word, nobody the wiser.

Unfortunately, an indiscretion on the part of that naughty little choirboy ruined everything.

The thing became known at the castle, and did little to improve the priest's reputation.

Several days later, new guests arrived.

I relinquished my room to Monsieur and Madame X..., and was moved into that of the children's tutor.

(I need not add that they didn't leave that young person, a lovely young woman, my word.)

That night, the heat was torrential, as Delcourt says, and I went to bed (violating all the health laws) with the window open.

I was engrossed in an affecting novel, *Carmen Lohry*, by Pierre Allen, when suddenly, framed by the window, a foreign body came between me and my view of the heavens.

This foreign body fell to the floor with a muffled thud.

A bouquet. In the bouquet, a letter.

Although I have a rather flattering idea of myself, I didn't think to attribute this aromatic message solely to my beauty.

The note was not meant for me, obviously, since I wouldn't be called a "cruel maiden." It was signed "Leo."

"Well, well, well," I murmured, with a knowing smile, "Mademoiselle tutor is wreaking havoc in poor men's hearts."

But who was Leo?

The next day, in my most careless tone, I said to Mademoiselle:

"I just saw Leo... He wanted me to tell you that he still loves you."

Mademoiselle blushed very deeply, and made no reply.

But that evening, after dinner, she took me aside:

"Because our parish priest told you about me, tell him that I can't stop him from being amorous, that's his right, but I do urge him to be more discreet."

What? Leo was the parish priest!

So, the following Sunday, I amused myself very much at mass.

Father Chamel delivered an indignant sermon on the increasing moral laxity among young people in the country.

When he had finished, I cried loudly:

"Bravo, Leo."

NOTES

"The End of a Collection" (*La fin d'une collection*): February 18, 1888, as *A l'oignon* ("With Onions"), with some differences.

A *motte* is a clump of earth; *faire boire la motte* means to put a dry clump into water.

A licitation is a sale by auction. The question mark is Allais's, who may have been unsure of the spelling, or wanted the reader to think he was.

"Disparatism" (*diparatisme*) is one of Allais's coinages (coinizations?)

Antonin Proust was a politician, painter, art critic, and friend of Manet. In 1890, he demanded the removal of a mosaic decoration on the Daru staircase in the Louvre, objecting that it was too garish.

"To speak like a Spanish cow" is an axiomatic critique of bad French.

"Chigneux": July 19, 1890, dated "Liverpool, July 16, 1890."

"Chigneux" means "crybaby"; a *coup d'oeil de travers* is a sideways glance.

Chigneux is a precursor of that later poacher Blaireau, in Allais's sole novel *L'Affaire Blaireau*. Never loath to reuse material, Allais lifted a few passages from this story for the fifth chapter.

Bistoquette is an old term for the penis.

Anatole Bérard des Glajeux was indeed a judge at the time. He was fond of Dostoevsky.

Toquard means "ridiculous, incompetent, ugly"; it covers a host of pejoratives that reflect poorly on the attorney, despite the extra C.

Jules Grévy was President from 1879 to 1887, after the resignation of Marshal Patrice de MacMahon. Grévy was known for his progressive policies, including abolition of capital punishment.

"Toussaint Latoquade": April 16, 1887, as *Dominique*; Toussaint Latoquade was originally named Dominique Saint-Père.

Our genial protagonist has an equally genial name: *Toussaint* is "All Saints' Day"; a *toquade* is a "whim" or "infatuation."

Cornélie Huss, née Pauss can only evoke Cornelius Nepos, a Roman historian whose simple style earned him a place in many Latin textbooks.

"Shocking": April 20, 1889, with a long introduction, cut for the book.

Sarah Vigott recalls *sa ravigote*. A ravigote is a seasoned sauce, either hot (velouté) or cold (vinaigrette). Its name proclaims it invigorating (from *ravigoter*).

Sarah Bernhardt was not only a famous actress, but a popular figure in Montmartre, and a friend of Allais's.

Blague means "joke," so Blagsmith must be a sort of blacksmith of jokes. He appears in several of Allais's stories.

"Stopover Romances" (*Amours d'escale*): April 11, 1891.

The island that Loti celebrated was Tahiti. Allais's fictional Lahila Islands are a pun on *la île là*, "the island there."

"Historia": November 7, 1891.

Historia sacerdotis bene finis seculi is dog Latin for "the story of a respectable fin-de-siècle priest."

Hautebeigne means something like "high slap."

In his first paragraph, Allais runs through the previous sixty years of French history: the reign of Charles X, from 1824 to 1830, who bankrupted the country with extravagant spending; the succession of Louis-Philippe, from the cadet branch of the Bourbons; the revolution of 1848; the tumultuous regime of Napoleon III in the Second Empire; the scandals of the Third Republic, in which President Jules Grévy's son-in-law Daniel Wilson sold memberships to the Legion of Honor; the fall of the populist politician Boulanger, who fled Paris to avoid arrest for treason and conspiracy, and eventually committed suicide on his mistress's grave.

"The Family of Alphonse of Gros-Caillou" is a rollicking song about a certain Alphonse, whose family attains wealth and respectability by running a whorehouse staffed by his sisters. Gros-Caillou is a neighborhood of Paris, in the seventh arrondissement.

The line of verse may be a quotation, possibly altered, but I can't trace it.

"Gioventù": February 28, 1891.

Gioventù, for the benefit of strict anglophones, means "youth" in Italian.

Peau-de-Lapin (Rabbit Skin) was a regular at the Café de la Nouvelle-Athènes, a dealer, apparently, in paintings and antiques. I found a mention of him in *Paris-Palette*, by Charles Virmaitre (1888): "The dealer in paintings is Peau-de-Lapin, a surname, hirsute head, good-hearted, obliging, mocking."

The Butte (the Hill) is another name for Montmartre.

La Gazette des coiffeurs seems to have sprung from Allais's imagination.

"The Bighorns" (*Les mouflons*): July 20, 1889; it was originally presented as an "Excerpt from the Bulletin of the Society of Biology."

The Loing is a river in central France; it is innocent of journalism.

Toutaleuil calls to mind *tout à l'oeil*, "everything free."

Tâtort would be *t'as tort*, "you're wrong"; *T'as tort, Victor!* is a rhyming tag, like the more popular *Tu parles, Charles!*

Ode la Dhuys is, for some reason, *eau de la duis*, "water from the levee"; Leroy-Datout is *le roi d'atout*, "the king of trumps."

Saint-Polyte would be Saint-Hippolyte; many places are named after the early theologian.

Dr. Charles-Édouard Brown-Séquard claimed to cure impotence with a serum made from dog and guinea pig testes, or with an oral preparation of monkey testes. He recurs in Allais's writings; unfortunately, the Brown-Séquard treatment was ineffective for Francisque Sarcey.

The Panther of Batignolles was a group of anarchists.

Jean-Camille Fulbert-Dumontel contributed to many papers, and wrote several books on animals.

Émile Bergerat's book, *La chasse au mouflon, ou Petit voyage philosophique en Corse* (*Hunting the Bighorn, or A Little Philosophical Voyage to Corsica*) had been published in 1891.

I suspect this "certain Cappaza" is the Corsican aeronaut Louis Capazza, who crossed the Mediterranean in 1886.

"Supply Train" (*Royal-Cambouis*): March 3, 1888, as *Dans l'train* ("In the Train"); it was thoroughly reworked for the book.

The French title is stubbornly untranslatable: *royal-cambouis* is military slang for a soldier serving in the supply train. Literally it would be "royal oily," for they were notoriously both proud and filthy.

Puyrâleaux is, perhaps, "mount miser."

Plumard may have been slothful; his name means "bed."

Leboult de Montmachin is, I'm afraid, *le bout de mon machin*: "the end of my thing."

"The Sprinkler" (*L'arroseur*): April 3, 1886, as *Printemps* ("Spring").

Gaston was originally Gaëtan.

"The Homicidal Autograph" (*L'autographe homicide*): June 5, 1886, as *Fatale passion*, with some differences.

Courbevoie is a densely populated commune, just outside Paris.

Bonaventure Desmachins seems to be "the fortune of things."

Le Guillotiné persuadé is a short story by Eugène Charette, from 1862: a condemned man refuses to be guillotined, but is talked into it by a city official.

Auguste Nélaton was a physician and surgeon, best known for inventing a probe to find imbedded bullets.

Philippe Ricord was another physician; as you may have gathered from the context, he specialized in venereal diseases.

"Corydor" (*Colydor*): October 16, 1886, as *Le mariage de Saint-Polyte*, with some differences, including the the fact that Colydor was originally named Saint-Polyte.

Manille was one of the most popular card games at the time; the fact that ten is highest is one of the cardinal rules.

"Lighthouses" (*Phares*): October 11, 1890.

There is, really, a lighthouse in Fatouville, which guides ships on the estuary of the Seine.

Maurice O'Reilly was a journalist and regular at the Chat Noir. He accompanied Allais and George Auriol on a riotous trip to England that year.

Henry Somm was a painter, illustrator, and journalist; he showed with the Impressionists, and wrote at least one play for the Chat Noir.

Georges Lorin, also known as Cabriol, was a painter and cartoonist; he caricatured Allais for *L'Hydropathe*.

Pierre Delcourt was a writer who contributed to the rich variety of

Parisian journalism.

Livarot is proverbially stinky, the Limburger of French culture.

"Russian Crime" (*Crime russe*): November 1, 1884, as *Erreur*, with a number of differences.

I have, with some misgiving, substituted "at the drop of a hat" for the original "speaking of boots" (*à propos de bottes*), an idiom more familiar to francophones than anglophones, and then made the necessary adjustments.

The General is apparently a "sack of flour" (*sac à farine*).

Nontron knives are still made, as they have been since the 15th century. They are, as the name indicates, made in Nontron; Châtellerault is famous for its firearms.

Nini, if you were wondering, is named after the city Nizhny Novgorod.

"News Items: Summer Squibs" (*Faits-divers: et d'été*)

Jacques Laffitte, according to legend, applied for a job at a bank when he was twenty-one, and was hired on the spot when he picked up a pin in the courtyard. He went on to hold many administrative positions, including Governor of the Bank of France.

Edmond Q... sounds suspiciously like *et de mon cul*, "and of my ass."

Mazagran, by the way, is sweetened black iced coffee, served in a glass.

"Drum Class" (*L'école des tambours*): January 2, 1892.

Captain Lemballeur appears in a few of Allais's military stories. He is an *emballeur*: literally a "packager," idiomatically a "cop."

Larigouille presumably likes to se *rigouiller*, "amuse himself"; and Pelotuex must enjoy *peloter*, "to caress."

Lady Namitt would be pronounced *la dynamite*, which suggests Jane Avril's equally explosive nickname, *La Mélinite*.

Paul Déroulède was a fervent nationalist, writer of patriotic verse, ardent antisemite, and founder of the Ligue des Patriotes.

"Tom"

Toutaleuil, the site of "The Bighorns," returns; it still means "everything free."

A *sarbacane* is a "blowgun." Maybe it was those piercing eyes.

"And the last nine!" is not only a common exclamation in piquet, but an 1889 monologue by Allais's colleague George Auriol: a boy is so used to hearing his uncle shout the phrase in cafes, that he repeats it whenever anyone counts to eight, leading to trouble with his parents.

Paul Marrot was a journalist and poet; the verses are from his poem *Train de retour* ("Return Train").

Vae soli! is from Ecclesiastes 4:10: "Woe to him that is alone!"

"In Another Man's Skin" (*Dans la peau d'un autre*). This story formed the basis of a curious novel by Jehan Soudan, published in 1907 as a collaboration with Allais, with an apparently spurious letter from Allais.

A *sergent fourrier* is a quartermaster sergeant. *Sâr* was a supposedly Assyrian honorific assumed by the occultist Joséphin Péladan, who started a rather rackety Rosicrucian-Chaldean-Catholic-Wagnerian order that made quite a splash at the time. He was roundly mocked by Allais and his circle.

René François Armand Prudhomme, better known as Sully Prudhomme, put out his first collection of poetry, *Stances et poèmes*, in 1865. It contained his most famous poem, *Le vase brisé*, "The Broken Vase."

Paul Auguste Marie Adam was a novelist, allied with the Symbolists.

Down There (*Là-bas*) is a novel by Joris-Karl Huysmans, published in 1891, containing much ado about Satanism.

Harry Covayre recalls *haricot vert,* "green bean."

Epouvantibile visu is dog Latin for "frightening to see," a variation on the common tag *horribile visu.*

"Consolatrix": March 31, 1886, as *Conte de semaine sainte* ("Story for Holy Week").

Paul Harel was a poet, very attached to his native town of Échaffour, in Normandy. I don't know if the verse is his; I couldn't find it.

The quotation from Alfred de Musset is from his 1842 poem *Rappelle-toi* ("Remember").

Gaston Villemer and Lucien Delormel wrote an astonishing number of popular songs together, usually in the patriotic vein. I assume they wrote this one; the title has been used by several other songwriters.

The Salt Herring (*le Hareng-Saur*) was named after the popular recitation by Allais's friend, Charles Cros.

Perhaps Puyjûteux is related to Puyrâleux, in "Supply Train." He is, at any rate, "mount juicy."

"Foolishness" (*Loufoquerie*): September 20, 1890, as *Labadens* ("Alumni"); it was entirely rewritten for the book.

Edmond Tirouard derives, no doubt, from *et de mon tiroir* "and from my drawer," which may explain Allais's compositional method here.

The Impasse de Guelma (rechristened Villa de Guelma in 1986) is a short dead-end street in the 18th arrondissement in Paris.

"Post Office" (*Postes et télégraphes*): August 14, 1886, as *La télégraphiste,* with some differences.

Baisemoy-en-Cort means *baise-moi encore,* "kiss me again."

An *enfileur* is either a "card cheat" or a "homosexual," although, of course, the two are not mutually exclusive.

Coquelin Cadet (Ernest Alexandre Honoré Cadet) popularized the monologue in Parisian cabarets. Allais wrote several for him.

"Horse's Ass" (*Pète-sec*): October 10, 1885, as *Mon lieutenant...!*, with many differences.

Duveau is a *pète-sec*, literally a "dry farter," idiomatically a "harsh taskmaster." I think he also qualifies as a horse's ass. He is also a fool, a *veau*.

A *tocard* is a "loser," an "incompetent."

Hondiret is *on dirait*, "one would say."

Jules Guérin was an actor, a member of the Comédie-Française, and a journalist, particularly for *Gil Blas*.

The *Chass' d'Af'* is the *Chasseurs d'Afrique*, a light cavalry corps stationed in Africa.

"A Malcontent" (*Un mécontent*): February 23, 1889: it was published as a chapbook by Ollendorff that year, with the subtitle "A Monologue for Coquelin Cadet."

Fortuné and *bidard* both mean "lucky."

"The Postscript" (*Le post-scriptum*)

"To part, is to die a little" (*Partir, c'est mourir un peu*) is a line from Edmond Haraucourt's 1890 poem *Rondel de l'adieu* ("Rondel of farewell"). Allais added on another occasion, "But to die, is to part a lot."

I believe Michel makes some kind of amaro, but Curaçao is usually not a German product.

The colonel's name is *il y a du rabiot*, "there's some extra." Pourd-sur-Alaure is *pour sur alors*, "sure enough, then."

Colonel Ramollot was a hard-drinking, swaggering bully in a series of stories by Charles Leroy. Leroy, incidentally, was Allais's brother-in-law, having married Mathilde Allais.

"A New Boating": November 24, 1888, as *Petits bateaux* ("Little Boats"); it was originally dedicated to Georges Montorgueil, that is, Octave Lebesgue, journalist and author of children's books.

Tilia europaea, Linn. is linden tea.

Sainte-Anne is a psychiatric hospital in the 14th arrondissement.

The Divan Japonais was a cabaret in the Pigalle district. In 1891, it produced an operetta Allais wrote with Jules Desmarquoy, *Le Moulin de la Galette.*

Jean-Martin Charcot was a neurologist, particularly interested in hysteria and hypnosis.

Alfred Gervais was a French admiral. In 1891, his fleet visited the Russian fleet in Finland, and also sailed to Norway and Sweden.

The passage Alfred-Stevens is a passageway in the 9th arrondissement.

François Bidel was an animal trainer and menagerie director.

I suspected Faridjé was a real person, and managed to track her down. According to an article in *Le Figaro* (September 23, 1890) by *Un Badaud* (Hugues Le Roux), Faridjé was a dancer, and Bidel's niece. There was a movement to forbid female dancers in fairs, on the usual grounds of immorality, and Le Roux came to her defense.

"The Language of the Flowers" (*Le langage des fleurs*): September 13, 1890.

A *gourde* is a "fool," preferably a clumsy one.

The Queen of Romania, Elizabeth of Wied, wrote voluminously in several languages under the name of Carmen Sylva.

The Saint-Lazare station in Paris was, at the time, one of the main terminals of the railway line l'Ouest.

Charles Ephrussi was a wealthy art critic and collector.

Léon Armand Charles de Baudry d'Asson was a contentious politician, who made a career of attacking Jews and Freemasons, and upholding Catholicism.

"Bébert": April 9, 1887.

Bébert is a diminutive for Robert or Albert.

Charles Chincholle was a prolific journalist, novelist, humorist, and playwright.

"Miousic": January 12, 1889, as *L'orgue* ("The Organ").

Montmorency, near Paris, is famed for its cherries.

François les Bas-Bleus is a comic opera by Ernest Dubreuil, Eugène Humbert, Paul Burani, Firmin Bernicat, and André Messager. *Espérance en d'heureux jours* was the big number in the second act.

"The Profitable Absence" (*L'absence profitable*): September 18, 1886, as *L'avancement* ("The Promotion"), with some differences.

Constant Lejaune is "constant the cuckold."

Ary-Golade is an unusual spelling of *à rigolade*, "for laughs."

❋ ❋ ❋

EXTRA STORIES

"By Analogy" (*Par analogie*): August 27, 1887.

A *caron* is a "piece of lean bacon"; a *creux*, a "hollow."

"Pretty Polly" (*Vert-Vert*): December 17, 1887.

Vert-Vert is the title character in the poem *Vert-Vert, ou les Voyages du perroquet de la Visitation de Nevers* ("Green-Green, or the Travels of the Parrot from the Visitation of Nevers"), by Jean-Baptiste Gresset (1734). The plot, if you can call that, revolves around a parrot squawking obscenities in a convent.

Séverine was the pen name of Caroline Rémy, anarchist, feminist, and journalist.

"Delicacy" (*Délicatesse*): January 14, 1888.

Henri Rivière was an artist, best known for his woodcuts and lithographs, often influenced by Japanese prints. More pertinently here, he originated the shadow plays at the Chat Noir, and was on the staff of the paper.

The "Translator's note" given as a footnote is Allais's, not mine.

"The Parish Priest" (*Monsieur le curé*): March 17, 1888.

Colonel Charles-Ragan de Bange invented the cannon that bears his name, and which is still popular among slaughter buffs.

Chamel is an archaic variant of *chameau*, literally "camel," but figuratively "scoundrel." More importantly, however, abbé Chamel evokes béchamel, the beloved white sauce.

Ventrouilly (Yonne-Inférieure) sounds a lot like *ventrouille en inférieur*, "bow like an inferior."

Chamel's skill with a rod is reminiscent of Nimrod, who was a mighty hunter before the Lord (Genesis 10:9).

Jules Roques founded and edited the satirical weekly *Le Courrier Français*, to which Allais contributed a few stories. It was also notable for devoting entire issues to the Incohérents, the proto-dada art exhibits where Allais showed his all-white picture, *First Communion of Chlorotic Girls in a Snowstorm*.

The Delcourt is probably Pierre Delcourt, mentioned above in "Lighthouses."

Carmen Lohry was published in 1887, and has left little trace. I did find a blurb in the *Revue Illustrée* for July 1, 1887, which describes it as "the intimate struggle of love against duty, the natural union of two passionate souls." Pierre Allen was one of the pen names of Paul Toutain, a childhood friend of Allais's, who usually wrote under the pseudonym Jean Revel.

ABOUT THE AUTHOR

ALPHONSE ALLAIS (1854 – 1905) began his career in Paris during the Belle Epoque. He was particularly active at the legendary cabaret Le Chat Noir, where he wrote for and edited the weekly paper. He quickly became known for his deadpan wit and inexhaustible imagination. Among other things, he also exhibited some of the first monochromatic pictures (such as his all-white "First Communion of Chlorotic Girls in the Snow" in 1883) and composed the first silent piece of music: "Funeral March for the Obsequies of a Deaf Man" (1884).

Throughout most of his life, he contributed columns several times a week to *Le Journal* and *Le Sourire*. These pieces were collected into twelve volumes, which he called his "Anthumous Works," between 1892 and 1902. He also published a collection of his monochromes, *Album Primo-Avrilesque*, in 1897, and a novel, *L'Affaire Blaireau*, in 1899, as well as a few plays. His later years were troubled by debt, a bad marriage, and heavy drinking; he died at 59.

He was a crucial influence on Alfred Jarry, as well as on the Surrealists: Breton included him in his *Anthology of Black Humor*, and Duchamp was reading him on the day he died. Allais's fascination with wordplay, puns, and holorhymes led Oulipo to call him an "anticipatory plagiarist"; the Pataphysical College dubbed him their "Patacessor." His books have remained in print in France, and the Académie Alphonse Allais has awarded a literary prize in his honor since 1954.

ABOUT THE TRANSLATOR

Doug Skinner has contributed articles and cartoons to *Black Scat Review, Oulipo Pornobongo, The Fortean Times, Strange Attractor Journal, Fate, Weirdo, The Anomalist, Nickelodeon, Cabinet,* and other fine publications. Black Scat has published several books of his stories and cartoons, as well as his translations of the French humorist Alphonse Allais.

He has written music for several dance companies, including ODC-San Francisco and Margaret Jenkins; his scores for actor/clown Bill Irwin include *The Regard of Flight, The Courtroom, The Regard Evening,* and *The Harlequin Studies.* He has performed his songs in many theaters, clubs, and cabarets. His puppet shows with Michael Smith have been seen everywhere from Caroline's Comedy Club in Manhattan to the Museum of Contemporary Art in Los Angeles.

TV and movie appearances include *Great Performances, The '90s, Martin Mull's Talent Takes a Holiday, Ed, Crocodile Dundee II,* and a smattering of commercials.

He lived for decades in Manhattan, but has moved to New Paltz, a few miles to the north.

The Alphonse Allais Collection
Published by Black Scat Books

"... one of the great masterpieces of humorous literature."
—*nooSFere Littérature*

"...apart from being long-awaited, *Captain Cap* also comes at a timely moment because its ironies are particularly apposite today as we witness global intellectual colonization." — *Leonardo Reviews*

Translated and with an introduction, notes, and illustrations by Doug Skinner, this is the complete, unabridged text of the original 1902 French classic by the peerless humorist, Alphonse Allais. This deluxe edition also features eight uncollected "Captain Cap" stories, plus a "Cappendix" of rare historical pictures. Over 360 pages of absurdist mirth and howls of laughter.

This collection of Allais's rare theatrical texts includes original translations—never before published in English—of ten monologues, three one-act plays, and twelve shorter dialogues, skits and burlesques drawn from his columns in such publications as **Le Chat Noir** and **L'Hydropathe**. This delightful compilation by Doug Skinner (with fascinating notes on the texts) is proto-Dada at its most delicious.

"No Oulipian could fail to be enchanted by his essentially ironic tales, in which he juggles the rhetorical and narrative components of writing with rigorous logic and inexhaustibly zany results." —Harry Mathews

"Allais comes across as a very modern writer, and his work as an experimental enterprise which is exemplary in many ways... it is also quite possible to invoke such writers as Queneau, Calvino, and Borges." —Jean-Marie Defays

Belly laughs guaranteed!

Here is the master absurdist's inaugural collection, containing his hand-picked favorites from the pages of Le Chat Noir, the bohemian journal that amused and scandalized Paris. Here you'll find Allais in the first flush of his comic genius, spinning out elegant and hilarious gems of black humor on suicide, murder, obsession, and adultery. You will meet the philosophical cuckold, the young lady in love with a pig, the inventor of the Tumultoscope, and Ferdinand, the most resourceful duck in literature. Among the highlights is Allais's most famous story, "A Thoroughly Parisian Drama," a favorite of André Breton and Umberto Eco. This is the book's first publication in English, and features seven additional stories from **Le Chat Noir**, as well as a sublime introduction, notes on the text, and drawings by Doug Skinner.

Alphonse Allais's elegance, scientific curiosity, preoccupation with language and logic, wordplay and flashes of cruelty inspired Alfred Jarry, as well as succeeding generations of Surrealists, Pataphysicians, and Oulipians. **The Squadron's Umbrella** collects 39 of his funniest stories — many originally published in the legendary paper **Le Chat Noir**, written for the Bohemians of Montmartre. Included are such classic pranks on the reader as "The Templars" (in which the plot becomes secondary to remembering the hero's name) and "Like the Others" (in which a lover's attempts to emulate his rivals lead to fatal but inevitable results.).

As the author promises, this book contains no umbrella and the subject of squadrons is "not even broached."

"... effervescent and flavorful, perfect in its way."

—*Wuthering Expectations*

Adapted to film four times, **L'Affaire Blaireau** has remained popular and in print in France since its original appearance in 1899. This is its first publication in English. It is humorist Alphonse Allais's only novel and, in the words of translator Doug Skinner: "It isn't quite as wild or cruel as his early stories, but I find it delicious anyway. Summer in the provinces, the shrewd but impressionable Blaireau, futile political squabbles, a ridiculous but charming love story, what more could one want? And innocence is rewarded!" Indeed, this novel is a rare find to be savored by the author's growing circle of fans in America

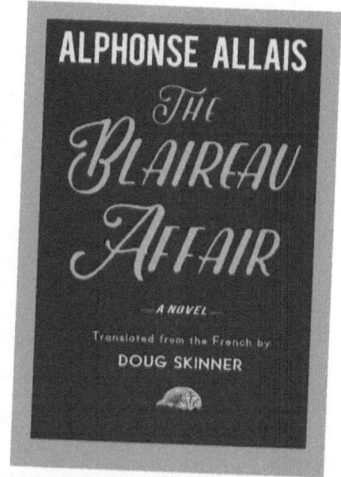

"...the unexpected is suddenly present, and there is rudeness, as well as a savagery of attack that we simply can't imagine anyone doing to any well-known columnist of today and getting away with it."

—Jeff Bursey

Alphonse Allais transforms the conservative French drama critic Francisque Sarcey into an Ubuesque piñata in a series of columns published under Sarcey's name, in the newspaper **Le Chat Noir**. The pseudo-Sarcey becomes a prattling idiot, bragging about his appetite and complaining about his impotence, a memorable comic character who often eclipsed the original. This sustained journalistic prank — compiled and translated by Doug Skinner — is a classic of black humor.

"Absurdism in all its glory....Anyone who wants to learn invaluable information about Sarcey's love for young women, the weather at the end of the 19th century (which seems surprisingly similar to that of today), his love of food (and doubtful vegetarianism) or his beloved umbrella, is highly advised to read I Am Sarcey." —Edith Doove

 Visit BlackScatBooks.net

www.ingramcontent.com/pod-product-compliance
Lightning Source LLC
Chambersburg PA
CBHW021011180626
46814CB00003B/1236